FIRST PRINCIPLES OF CARD PLAY

Paul Marston

faber and faber

LONDON · BOSTON

First published in Australia in 1986
by Hamilton Publishing Company
This revised edition
first published in Great Britain in 1990
by Faber and Faber Limited
3 Queen Square London WCIN 3AU

Printed in Great Britain by
Richard Clay Limited Bungay Suffolk

A CIP record for this book is available
from the British Library
ISBN 0–571–14443–8

CONTENTS

PREFACE

This book covers the elements of card play. It assumes that you have played a little bridge, enough to know how the game works. So far you may have concentrated on your bidding but now you would like to play the cards well, both as declarer and defender.

What a good position to be in! For a reasonable amount of effort you can directly improve your results. While each hand may occur as infrequently as Halley's Comet, most hands can be categorised and you will see the same old problems time after time.

This means that you can be a successful card player without having a computer brain; you do not have to memorise endless figures. Just learn how to use a short list of principles and you will be well on the way. Five percent of the hands may be complex but the rest are not.

This book shows you how to play well on the straightforward ninety-five percent of the hands. It reveals the principles that constantly recur, then it demonstrates by example how you can take advantage of them.

Most of the examples are "step by step". That is, you are asked questions and given the answers as you play through the hands. Do take the trouble to work out your own answers. It is more effective if you work them out for yourself.

I have watched many players go through the process of acquiring these skills, and no-one has had to concede defeat. Admittedly it sometimes takes an effort, but they think it was well worthwhile.

It will surely be the same for you. By the end of the book you will play with confidence and purpose. You will take more tricks both in play and defence.

SECTION 1

PLAY IN NOTRUMPS

INTRODUCTION

When partner presents you with dummy, there is a maze of possibilities, yet the same few principles apply. In this section you will learn about those that apply in notrumps. They are very important because they can be used on almost every single hand.

First you will find out how tricks are made. This is the subject of the first four chapters. Although this section is about notrumps, you will often use the same plays in suit contracts and on defence.

Having refined your trick-taking technique, the remaining chapters concentrate on the hand as a whole. They look at the problems of planning, getting backwards and forwards, as well as dealing with your scheming opponents. The two following sections of this book assume that you know about notrumps.

As you are reading through the step-by-step hands it is a good idea to cover the following text with a piece of paper. In spite of the most honest will, it is easy to glance at the answers if they are on view.

Chapter 1
CERTAIN TRICKS

> **In this chapter you will learn what certain tricks are, how to count them, how to *cash* them and how to overcome blockages.**

A certain trick is one that can be taken without losing the lead. An ace is worth one certain trick and an ace-king in the same suit is worth two. If you also hold the queen in that suit you have three tricks and so on. A king without the ace is not a certain trick.

Whenever you become the declarer your first move should be to count your certain tricks. How many certain tricks do you have in each of these combinations?

Example 1:1 Counting certain tricks.

1. **You**   **Dummy**
   ♠ K 7 6   ♠ A 5 3

2. **You**   **Dummy**
   ♠ K J   ♠ A Q

3. **You**   **Dummy**
   ♠ K Q 5   ♠ A 6

4. **You**   **Dummy**
   ♠ K J 8 5   ♠ A Q 7

In counting tricks you must remember that one card is played from both hands on each trick.

In combination one you have two certain tricks, the ace and the king.

In combination two you still have only two tricks because although you have the four top cards in the suit your longest holding in the suit is only two cards. So you can only play two rounds.

Combination three is similar to combination two except that you have an extra card in your hand and you can therefore make an extra trick, that is three in all.

In combination four you can make four tricks.

Note that these examples would be no different if the dummy hand and yours were swapped.

In studying the examples you may find it helpful to use real cards. It may take a little time to set up the problems but if it helps you to understand the positions it is worthwhile.

Making certain tricks takes no special talent. All the same, the order in which the cards are played can be vital:

Example 1:2 Unblocking.

You	Dummy
♠ K 2	♠ A Q 3

You have three tricks, but there is a danger that you will *block* the suit. That is, you will have tricks ready to be taken but the lead will be in the wrong hand.

What you should do is play the honour from the shorter holding first, in this case the king. Then play the two to the ace and queen. If you make the mistake of playing the ace or the queen on the first round you will block the suit. The king will take the second trick leaving the lead in your hand with the third winner stranded in dummy.

3

PLAY THE HONOURS FROM THE SHORTER HAND FIRST

In these five examples, which card would you play on the first lead of the suit so that you can take all your tricks?

Example 1:3 Cashing certain tricks.

1. **You** **Dummy**
   ♡ K 8 ♡ A Q 6

2. **You** **Dummy**
   ♢ A Q J 4 ♢ K 8

3. **You** **Dummy**
   ♡ Q J 3 2 ♡ A K 7

4. **You** **Dummy**
   ♣ A K 8 ♣ Q J 7 5

5. **You** **Dummy**
   ♣ K Q J 7 ♣ A 4

With one and two you should play the king first, with three and four the ace-king, and with five the ace should be played first.

OVERTAKING

When you have bare honours, you will have to do more than play the honours from the shorter holding first, if you are to *cash* all your tricks in a suit. (To cash means to take a trick with a certain winner.)

When your honours are bare, you should overtake your own trick to get the lead in the right hand, if you can afford to. This is how:

Example 1:4 Overtaking dry honours.

1.	You	Dummy
	♠ K J	♠ A Q 5

2.	You	Dummy
	♠ A J 7	♠ K Q

3.	You	Dummy
	♡ A Q	♡ K J 10 5

4.	You	Dummy
	♠ K J 3	♠ A Q

5.	You	Dummy
	◇ K 10 6 5	◇ A Q J

1. Play the king and overtake the jack to enable you to cash three tricks.
2. Cash the king (or queen) and overtake the other honour with the ace to cash the jack.
3. Cash the ace and overtake the queen to put the lead where you want it.
4. Take the ace and overtake the queen.
5. Take the ace-queen and then overtake the jack with the king to cash the ten.

A variation of this situation occurs when you have a bare honour opposite strength — say AQJ opposite the king by itself. Lead the king and overtake with the ace to put the lead in the hand with the extra winners.

BLOCKAGES
Sometimes you will not have the strength in the suit to allow you to overtake. The suit is then said to be *blocked*. This means that your tricks in the suit cannot be taken one after another. In this case you should cash the bare honours as soon as possible to clear the way. For example:

Example 1:5 Hopelessly blocked.

1. **You**   **Dummy**
   ♠ A 4 3   ♠ K Q

2. **You**   **Dummy**
   ♠ Q J 8   ♠ A K

In one you cannot afford to overtake the second round of spades to put the lead in your hand because you do not have the jack. You must therefore cash the king and queen and later, when the lead is in your hand, take the ace. With two the suit is hopelessly blocked. You must take the ace-king and play another suit. Later, you may be able to cash the queen.

Example 1:6 Short honour first.

Contract: 3NT	**You**	**Dummy**
Lead: ♠ K	♠ A 5 2	♠ J 4
	♡ A 7 6 5	♡ 9 3 2
	◇ K 2	◇ A Q J 10 3
	♣ A K 8 6	♣ 7 4 3

HOW MANY CERTAIN TRICKS DO YOU HAVE?
One spade, one heart, five diamonds, and two clubs. That is enough for your contract.

HOW WILL YOU PLAY THE DIAMONDS?
The only possible pitfall is in the diamond suit. You have no side entry to the dummy so it is vital that you play the honours in the proper order.

The king should be played first then the small one led across to the dummy. If you incorrectly win the king of diamonds on the second round you will be unable to reach your three remaining diamond winners.

How do you play this three notrump contract?

Example 1:7 Short honour then overtake.

Contract: 3NT	You	Dummy
Lead: ♠ K	♠ 9 8 3	♠ A 4 2
	♡ A K 6	♡ 9 7 3
	◇ A 9 7 3	◇ J 2
	♣ A Q J	♣ K 10 8 5 2

HOW MANY CERTAIN TRICKS DO YOU HAVE?
One spade, two hearts, one diamond, and five clubs. You have nine tricks and all you must do is be careful to take them all.

HOW WILL YOU PLAY THE CLUBS?
The spade lead will take away your only entry to dummy outside the club suit so you must make sure you do not block the suit. The correct play is to cash the ace and the queen (or jack) then overtake the last remaining honour with the king in dummy to allow you to cash the rest of the suit.

IMPORTANT POINTS TO REMEMBER
1. A certain trick is one that can be taken without giving up the lead.
2. In counting your certain tricks, remember a card must be played from **both** hands on each trick.
3. The first step in playing a hand is to count the certain tricks.
4. In cashing the certain tricks play the honours from the hand with the least cards in the suit, first.
5. When the shorter hand has no small card, only honours, you may be able to overtake the last honour so that the lead is in the longer hand.

Chapter 2
TRICKS BY PROMOTING
SECONDARY HONOURS

In this chapter you will learn how to make winners
from secondary honours, and in which order to play
these cards. You will learn how to count these tricks
and when to give up the lead.

The king, queen, jack, and ten are secondary honours. Successful
card play is not simply a matter of cashing certain tricks. You must
also create tricks with your secondary honours. The most basic
technique for trick development is *promotion*.

PROCESS OF PROMOTION
When a high card is played all the smaller cards move up one rank.
When the ace is played, the king becomes boss and the queen
number two and so on. *Establishing* tricks by promotion is the
process of forcing out the opponents' high cards so that your
secondary honours become winners.

TOUCHING HONOURS

Promoting tricks is easiest when you have *touching* honours. That is, honours that are next to each other in rank. For example, the king and queen are adjacent and therefore touching. So too are the jack-ten-nine.

Honours may also be touching if the honour(s) in between have been played. The ace and queen are touching if the king has been played. It is not necessary for the honours to be in the same hand. They are still touching if they are divided between your hand and dummy. Touching honours are sometimes known as *equal honours* or just *equals*.

A run of two or more touching honours is called a *sequence*. A sequence is a valuable asset. It is a good source of tricks when you are playing the hand and it offers an attractive lead when you are defending.

To illustrate the value of touching honours, imagine you hold the king in dummy and only small cards in your hand. If you lead the king it will be taken by the ace. With the departure of the king goes any chance of winning a trick in the suit. If, however, you also held the touching honour, the queen, it would now be promoted to winning rank.

Touching honours are a good source of tricks because chance does not play a part. You simply lead one of the touching honours to force out the opposition's winners and relentlessly promote your remaining honours.

Example 2:1 Counting promoted tricks.

You	Dummy
◇ 7 4 3	◇ K Q J

You have no certain tricks because you do not have the ace, but you can promote two tricks by leading one of your honours and forcing out the ace. The ace may not be taken immediately but that does not affect how many tricks you can take.

Work out how many tricks you can establish with each of these holdings:

Example 2:2 How many promoted tricks?

1. **You**   **Dummy**
   ♡ 5 3 2   ♡ Q J 10

2. **You**   **Dummy**
   ◇ Q 4   ◇ K J 10 7

3. **You**   **Dummy**
   ♣ J 10 9 8   ♣ 7 4 3

4. **You**   **Dummy**
   ♠ Q 9   ♠ J 10 6 3

1. You can establish one trick. Lead the queen to force out the king. On regaining the lead, play the jack to force out the ace leaving your ten best.

2. You can establish three tricks. Force out the ace and you have three winning cards in dummy. Note, you should play the queen first according to the principle mentioned in chapter one; play the honour from the shorter holding first, to unblock the suit. This principle is just as important when promoting tricks as it is when taking certain tricks.

3. You can establish one trick in due course. It may not look like trick-taking material but it is. Play the jack forcing out the queen. Then the ten to drive out the king, and the nine to clear the ace and guess what, your eight is best.

4. This time you can establish two tricks. Play the queen (honours from the shorter holding first), then the nine, leaving the jack-ten in dummy best.

SOLID HOLDINGS
The best sort of suit holding is one that is *solid*. **A solid suit contains nothing but winning cards.** For example, if you have the ace-king-queen in a suit it is solid. All your cards are winners

and none are losers. A suit can become solid by promotion. For example, K Q J opposite 6 4 3 is not solid because the ace is missing, but if you lead the king and the opposition take the ace the remaining Q J opposite 6 4 **are** solid.

ESTABLISH YOUR TRICKS EARLY

The typical approach of inexperienced card players is to grab every trick in sight, before losing the lead. Maybe this is caused by the painful memory of going "to bed" with top cards after innocently giving up the lead, or perhaps it is simply because they can think of nothing better to do. Whatever the reason, do not fall victim to this mistaken way of thinking. **The proper approach is to establish your tricks as early as possible, which means you must give up the lead early in the hand.** It is very important that you do this.

DO NOT BE AFRAID TO LOSE THE LEAD

CONTROL AND ITS IMPORTANCE

You control a suit when you hold the top card in that suit. If you hold the second or third best card in the suit you are said to have secondary control.

When you have control of a suit you can stop the opponents from taking tricks in that suit. Thus, your opponents will try to drive out your controlling cards. Once you have been forced to play your controlling cards you are in danger of losing a number of tricks in the suit. This is why it is important to cling on to your controlling cards and only play them when you are forced to.

HOW TO TACKLE A COMPLETE DEAL

The first thing you should do is count your certain tricks. Why not the promoted tricks? Because plans to promote tricks can come unstuck. Take this example: Q J 5 opposite 10 9 4. You have to give the lead away twice to promote your trick. There is a danger that in losing the lead twice the opponents will be able to establish **their** suit and take enough tricks to defeat you.

When you are planning to promote tricks you should therefore bear in mind how many times you must lose the lead and you should be aware of what the opponents are threatening to do.

First you count your certain tricks so you will know how far you are short of your contract. Certain tricks usually provide only about half of your total needs. The next move is to work out where the extra tricks should come from. The most attractive source of extra tricks is a sequence, if you have one. In summary, you should:

1. **Count the certain tricks.**
2. **Find where to go for the extra tricks you need.**

Try out your planning on this hand. You are in three notrumps on the lead of the queen of spades. How would you play?

Example 2:3 Promoting touching honours.

Contract: 3NT	You	Dummy
Lead: ♠ Q	♠ K 6 5	♠ A 7 2
	♡ J 4 3	♡ A K 5
	◇ A K 9 5	◇ 8 7 2
	♣ K 10 3	♣ Q J 6 4

You have six certain tricks so you need three more. The club honours are touching and will provide three winners after you drive out the ace. You should win the king of spades and immediately play the king of clubs. In this way you establish your tricks while you still have control of the other suits. By correctly setting up your tricks early you will make your contract for sure. With luck you will make an overtrick (perhaps the queen of hearts will fall under the ace or king) but that is only icing on the cake. Your main job is to make your contract.

How would you go about playing three notrumps on this next hand? North leads the jack of spades.

Example 2:4 Choosing between two suits.

Contract: 3NT   **You**   **Dummy**

Lead: ♠ J
              ♠ A 4 2   ♠ K 8 3
              ♡ Q 6   ♡ K J 10 7 2
              ◇ A K 5   ◇ 8 4 3
              ♣ A 8 7 3 2   ♣ Q 6

HOW MANY CERTAIN TRICKS DO YOU HAVE?

Five: two spades, two diamonds, and one club. You need four more tricks and the obvious place to try is the heart suit because you have touching honours.

WHAT DO YOU PLAY AT TRICK ONE?

You need to establish four heart tricks so keep the entry to the dummy. Win the first trick with the ace of spades.

WHAT DO YOU PLAY AT TRICK TWO?

You should immediately begin work on establishing your tricks which means playing hearts.

WHICH HEART DO YOU PLAY?

The correct card is the queen, the honour from the shorter holding first. You will force out the ace of hearts and use the king of spades as an entry card to play off the promoted winners, leaving you with nine tricks in all.

As you know, with honours split between hand and dummy it is best to play the honour from the shorter holding first. When you have a choice of touching honours to play from hand, which should you play? For example, the KQJ. In one sense it does not matter because they are all *equal,* but in another it does. The opponents do not know about your strong holding and the best way to keep it a secret is to play the **top** card of the sequence. In this case, play the king.

This is not a major issue, just a small edge. Throughout this text it will be assumed that declarer will play the highest of touching honours, as much for brevity as the attendant camouflage.

Each hand requires fresh thought; what do you make of this hand? You are in three notrumps on the lead of a small club.

Example 2:5 Overtaking to promote.

Contract: 3NT	**You**	**Dummy**
Lead: ♣ 5	♠ A K Q 5	♠ 4 2
	♡ 7 4 3	♡ Q J 10
	◇ Q J	◇ K 10 9 8 7
	♣ 8 6 4 3	♣ A K 2

HOW MANY CERTAIN TRICKS DO YOU HAVE?
Just five: three spades and two clubs. The extra tricks should come from the diamond suit. You win the king of clubs. What do you do now? Okay, you should play on diamonds, but you have to be more specific.

HOW SHOULD YOU PLAY THE DIAMOND SUIT?
You must be careful not to block the suit. Play the queen and on the second round of the suit, whether the ace was taken or not, play the jack and overtake with the king. This ensures that you will not strand your diamond winners in dummy. Playing this way your contract is guaranteed.

If you do not overtake the second diamond, you will be defeated if the opposition does not win the ace of diamonds on either the first or second round of the suit. You would be unable to both establish the diamonds **and** enter dummy to take them.

IMPORTANT POINTS TO REMEMBER
1. Touching honours are those of adjacent rank. A run of two or more touching honours is called a sequence. Such holdings are a good source of extra tricks.
2. As declarer, play the top card from a sequence because it gives the opponents the least information.
3. Know how many tricks you need to establish.
4. Establish your tricks early.
5. Do not be afraid of losing the lead.
6. Keep controlling cards as long as you can.

Chapter 3
LONG SUIT TRICKS

In this chapter you will learn how to take tricks with the small cards. You will use long suits to set up small cards as winners.

Good players know how to make lots of tricks with small cards. If you hold the two of spades and the opponents have run out of the suit your two is a winner. This is an example of a long suit trick.

The low cards only take tricks when the opponents have run out of the suit. **You therefore need to hold the majority of the cards in the suit.** Consider this:

Example 3:1 Potential of small cards.

```
              North
              ♡ J 9 7
    You                    Dummy
    ♡ A K Q 4              ♡ 5 3 2
              South
              ♡ 10 8 6
```

You have three certain tricks but you can also make a *long suit* trick. Watch! The ace, king, and queen, draw three cards from each of the opponents (and dummy too). All the outstanding cards in the suits have been played so your four is promoted to winning status.

Long suit tricks will usually come from suits in which you hold the majority of the cards. Imagine you took the lowly two from dummy in the example above and gave it to North or South. No matter who you gave it to, it would not be possible for you to take more than your ace-king-queen. The player with the fourth card in the suit would be able to beat your four.

Example 3:2 Developing two long-suit tricks.

> **North**
> ♡ J 6 2

You   **Dummy**
♡ A K 8 7 3   ♡ Q 5 4

> **South**
> ♡ 10 9

Play low to the queen (honour from the shorter holding first) then back to the king and ace. Your three certain tricks in the suit have stripped the opponents of hearts so your two remaining small cards are winners.

HOW TO TELL WHEN SMALL CARDS ARE WINNERS

All you have to do is count the cards! This is not the tough task that non-bridge players tend to think it is. You do not have to count every suit. You simply concentrate on the suits that you are developing.

There are thirteen cards in each suit. What you must do is keep track of the number that have been played. When you want to know how many are left outstanding, add the number that have been played to the number you and dummy hold and subtract the total from thirteen. This is how many are outstanding. It may seem an effort at first because there are so many other things for you to think about, but persevere; in time it will become easy.

You can also establish suits that are very weak provided you have the length:

Example 3:3 Setting up a weak suit.

<pre>
                      North
                      ♡ K Q 9
You   Dummy
♡ 8 7 6 4 2   ♡ A 5 3
                      South
                      ♡ J 10
</pre>

You have one certain trick in this suit. You can establish two long suit tricks as well by losing the lead twice. Play to the ace drawing one card from each defender. Next give the opponents a trick in the suit. When next you win the lead, give them their last winner and your two remaining cards in the suit will be good.

You could take this a step further:

Example 3:4 A suit without honour.

<pre>
                      North
                      ♣ K Q 10
You   Dummy
♣ 9 8 7 6 4   ♣ 5 3 2
                      South
                      ♣ A J
</pre>

Each time you get the lead, play clubs. Play three rounds to force out the opposition's top cards and you will establish two long suit tricks for your perseverance. Notice that if North had either one of South's clubs, you could only establish one trick in the suit. You would have to lose the lead four times to do so.

17

THE BREAK OF SUITS

The way the outstanding cards are divided between the two opposition hands is usually important. Take this layout:

You   **Dummy**
♡ A K Q 4   ♡ 5 3 2

You have three certain tricks and you could make a long suit trick as well. There are six cards outstanding and it depends on how they divide. If each opponent holds three (this is called a 3-3 break) they will be drawn by the ace, king, queen, and the four in your hand will be a long suit winner.

If on the other hand the six missing cards are divided four in one hand and two in the other (this is called a 4-2 break), you cannot make a long suit trick. The opponent with four cards will guard the fourth round of the suit.

It is possible that the suit could be even more lopsided than this. For example, one player could hold five and the other one (a 5-1 break) or one player might hold all six (a 6-0 break). These uneven breaks, however, only occur one time in six.

CHOOSING BETWEEN TWO SUITS

With two suits that could provide long suit tricks, you must decide which one to back. There are two factors in this decision. Firstly, the number of tricks the suit is likely to provide, and secondly, the number of cards you have in the suit between the two hands. The most important factor is the length:

PLAY ON THE SUIT WITH THE MOST CARDS

The more cards you have in a particular suit the less the opposition has. When you have length it is easier to establish long suit tricks. Also, you are less likely to encounter a bad break. Take this example:

Example 3:5 Play the longest suit.

                        Dummy
                        ♠ K 4 3
                        ♡ A 5
West   **East**
♠ Q 9 7   ♠ J 10
♡ J 7   ♡ Q 10 9 3
                        You
                        ♠ A 8 6 5 2
                        ♡ K 8 6 4 2

Imagine you need to make four tricks from one of these suits.
Each suit has two certain tricks but one has a total of eight cards
and the other just seven. It is question of which suit is more likely
to break evenly. If either defender holds four of one of these suits
you cannot make four tricks from it. Which suit should you play?

   The defenders are more likely to hold four hearts than four
spades because they have **more of them.** With an otherwise equal
choice, play on the suit in which you hold most cards. In this case
play spades.

Time to play a hand or two. Your contract is three notrumps.
Plan the play on the lead of the queen of diamonds.

Example 3:6 Undeterred by a bad break.

Contract: 3NT	**You**	**Dummy**
Lead: ◇ Q	♠ Q 7 4	♠ K J 8 5 2
	♡ K 7 2	♡ A 9 3
	◇ K 3 2	◇ A 8 5
	♣ K 9 5 2	♣ A 4

HOW MANY CERTAIN TRICKS DO YOU HAVE?
Six. Two each in hearts, diamonds, and clubs.

WHERE WILL THE OTHER TRICKS COME FROM?

The spade suit. By driving out the opponents' ace you can promote four spade tricks as long as the suit breaks 3-2. After winning the king of diamonds you lead to the jack of spades which loses to the ace. The opponents lead another diamond which you take. When you play to the queen of spades, however, North *shows out*. This means he can no longer follow suit. Now the spade layout is fully exposed.

WHAT DO YOU PLAN TO DO NOW?

The division of the spades is unfortunate but not fatal. Take the king of spades, and give South his spade trick (he started with four to the ace-ten). You will lose two spades and two diamonds — assuming South has another diamond, but you have nine tricks: three spades, two hearts, two diamonds, and two clubs.

The 4-1 break meant you only made three rather than four spade tricks. But only three were needed for the contract. You would go down in this contract if you did not persist with the spades. Sometimes it is necessary to lose several tricks in a suit in order to promote extra tricks. Once again, do not be afraid to lose the lead.

Example 3:7 Setting up a weak suit.

Contract: 3NT	You	Dummy
Lead: ♠ J	♠ K 9 7	♠ A Q 5
	♡ A K 2	♡ 9 8 5
	◇ A K 4 2	◇ 7 3
	♣ 8 3 2	♣ A 10 7 5 4

HOW MANY CERTAIN TRICKS DO YOU HAVE?

Three spades, two hearts, two diamonds, and one club; a total of eight.

WHERE CAN YOU GET ANOTHER TRICK?
Only in the club suit. You will first have to give the opponents at least two tricks in the suit. If the suit breaks 3-2 you can promote two extra tricks by losing two. You would then make a total of ten tricks. If the club suit breaks 4-1, unlikely but possible, you must lose three tricks in order to make a trick out of dummy's fifth club.

WHAT IS YOUR PLAN?
You should win the spade lead in your hand. This keeps the spade honours as entries to dummy which has the long suit that is to be developed. After winning the king of spades, you should immediately lead clubs.

WHAT WOULD HAPPEN IF YOU TAKE SAY THE ACE AND KING OF DIAMONDS FIRST?
When the opponents got the lead as they surely will since you only have eight winners, they would cash the diamond tricks that you have helped them to promote. If one of the defenders started with a long diamond suit he may have enough promoted tricks to defeat you. If such a disaster befalls you, be very sure that you blame yourself and not some innocent party such as the opponents or *luck*.

IMPORTANT POINTS TO REMEMBER
1. Long suits are an asset because they provide you with long suit tricks.
2. Keep count of the cards that have gone in suits you are establishing. Subtract this number and those that you hold from thirteen for the number outstanding.
3. Establish the suit in which you hold the most cards. Seldom tackle suits where you hold less than seven cards.
4. Set up your long suits at the first opportunity, before you take your certain winners. This helps you to retain control.

Chapter 4
ESTABLISHING TRICKS BY FINESSING

In this chapter you will learn how to win tricks with unsupported secondary honours. You will learn what a finesse is and why it works. You will see why you lead up to strength and when you should lead honours.

So far, you have established secondary honours by leading touching honours to flush out the opposing high cards. This is fine when you have the cards, but what about when key honours are missing? When there are gaps in the suit which you have to develop you must take advantage of the fact that each play is made in turn.

You can enjoy an advantage by playing *after* a player. By doing this you can choose what to play according to what your opponent plays. This illustration shows how it works with you on the receiving end. The declarer is enjoying an advantage by playing after you.

Imagine you are West in this diagram:

Example 4:1 The finesse.

Dummy
♡ A Q

You
♡ K J

Declarer
♡ 5 led

Declarer leads the five, what should you play? If you play the jack declarer can play the queen from dummy *which will win*. Why? Because you have the king and you have already played to the trick. Okay, should you play the king? No, that is no good either because now declarer will play the ace from dummy and his queen will be a second trick. Face up to it, there is absolutely nothing you can do. You are being *finessed*, or more correctly, your king is being finessed.

HOW A FINESSE WORKS
Declarer finessed the queen, finessing against your king to make two tricks in the suit. What happened? Declarer took advantage of playing after you. By this simple expedient he took a trick with the queen even though the king was outstanding. You were helpless.

Look how different it is when dummy has the lead. If the ace is cashed you play low and capture the queen with your king on the second round; if the queen is led you win your king right then and there. The difference is that with dummy on lead *you* play after dummy and not the other way around.

POSITIONAL VALUE OF HONOURS
When you play unsupported (non-touching) honours you cannot be sure of success. The outcome depends on who has the missing cards and this you do not know until you play. The thing you must understand about the finesse is that it gives you a chance to take tricks but not a guarantee. How do you play this combination?

Example 4:2 Finessing the king.

You	Dummy
◊ 5 4	◊ K 8

You should lead from your hand and when North plays low, try the king in the hope that he has the ace. If he does he cannot stop you taking one trick. If he plays the ace on the first round you simply play low from dummy and take the king on the next round of the suit.

What about when South has the ace? In that case your king will be gobbled by the ace and you will make nothing. That is true, but you were never going to make a trick anyway. The main thing is that whenever North has the ace you win the trick that is due to you.

Sometimes you can repeat a finesse:

Example 4:3 Repeating a finesse.

You	Dummy
♡ 6 4 3	♡ A Q J

You correctly play a heart to the queen which wins. It looks like North has the king so to take full advantage you must get the lead into your hand with another suit and repeat the finesse.

Example 4:4 Two finesses against an ace.

You	Dummy
♠ 6 4 3	♠ K Q 5

You play a spade to the king which wins. If North has the ace you can make a second trick in the suit but the next lead must come from your hand, not dummy. Lead some other suit until the lead is in your hand then lead towards the remaining honour, the queen.

When your honours are not touching, lead from the weak hand towards the strong hand. That way, you play from the strong hand after one of the opponents has committed himself.

LEAD UP TO STRENGTH

As you have already seen, you can only afford to lead honours when you have touching honours. The same idea applies here:

Example 4:5 Finessing by leading an honour.

You	Dummy
♣ Q J 10	♣ A 6 3

You must play from your own hand. You hope that North has the missing honour, the king. Lead the queen and see what he plays. If he plays the king, win the ace and your jack and ten will be two further tricks. If instead he plays low you must finesse by playing low in dummy. This way you will take three tricks whenever North has the king.

This situation is very similar:

Example 4:6 Leading the jack to trap the queen.

You	Dummy
♡ J 10 2	♡ A K 3

Lead the jack and if North does not produce the queen, play low from dummy. You will make three tricks whenever North has the queen.

In both the previous examples it was correct to lead an honour because you held touching honours. Without this, you should follow the normal advice of leading towards the strength.

Do you get the picture? How do you play this?

Example 4:7 Scoring an unsupported queen.

You	Dummy
◇ Q 9 5	◇ A 4 3

You should cash the ace then lead towards the queen, following the principle of leading up to strength. It is futile to lead the queen because if North holds the king he will play it on the queen, destroying any chance of a second trick in the suit.

Do not confuse this position with the earlier one where you led the queen. Then you held the jack-ten as well.

TAKING FINESSES IN SUITS LED BY THE OPPONENTS

In the previous example, if North leads the suit you can be certain of two tricks by playing a low card from dummy. If South plays the king, your ace and queen are now tricks. If instead of the king, South plays a low card you can win the queen. The play would be no different if you had only a doubleton queen in hand. Look at this situation:

Example 4:8 Finessing the queen.

You	Dummy
♡ A 4 3	♡ Q 2

Here if South on your right leads the suit you should play the three to ensure two tricks. The situation is different, however, if North leads the suit. If you play the two South will play some middle card to force out your ace. On the next round, the now bare queen will lose to the king no matter who has it. What you must do to give yourself a chance to win a second trick in the suit is take a finesse. When North leads the suit you should play the queen, which will win the trick when North has the king.

FINESSING WITH TWO HONOURS MISSING

Finessing technique can still be used if there are two honours missing:

Example 4:9 A double finesse.

You	Dummy
♡ 6 4 3	♡ A Q 10

Play low to the ten. If it wins, organise for the lead to be in your hand and play low to the queen. You will succeed in making three tricks when North has both the king and jack. Note that it would not be good enough to lead to the *queen* on the first round. Even if North has the king-jack you would not make three tricks.

Example 4:10 Another double finesse.

You	Dummy
◇ A J 10	◇ 8 5 4

Play low to the jack which will probably lose to the king or queen. Later, play to the ten, finessing South for the other honour.

Like all trick establishment plays, finesses should be taken early while you still have control in the other suits. Another consideration is that of entries. Make sure you give yourself the chance to lead towards your high cards by having the lead in the appropriate hand.

Be careful on this hand. You are in three notrumps and North leads the jack of spades.

Example 4:11 Entries for finessing.

Contract: 3NT
Lead: ♠ J

You	Dummy
♠ A K 4	♠ 9 7 3
♡ A Q 2	♡ 8 4 3
◇ A 7 5	◇ 9 8 4
♣ K Q 9 8	♣ A 4 3 2

HOW MANY CERTAIN TRICKS DO YOU HAVE?
Two spades, one heart, one diamond, and three clubs. Despite your wonderful hand the total is only seven.

WHERE CAN THE OTHER TWO TRICKS COME FROM?
There is a very good chance that the club suit will divide 3-2 allowing you to make a fourth trick in the suit. Your only chance for a ninth trick is by taking the finesse against the king of hearts. Suppose you now lead the king of clubs, followed by the queen and ace, the suit dividing 3-2 as you hoped. Now you could play a fourth round of clubs or take a heart finesse.

WHICH DO YOU CHOOSE?

If you mistakenly play a fourth round of clubs you will have no option but to win in your hand. This would put you in the wrong hand for the heart finesse. The ace of clubs is very definitely the only entry to dummy. You must therefore make good use of it and lead a heart. You have to get into the habit of thinking ahead. Good play comes from good planning.

How do you play this three notrump contract on the lead of the queen of clubs?

Example 4:12 Finessing without danger.

Contract: 3NT	You	Dummy
Lead: ♣ Q	♠ A Q 3	♠ 7 4 2
	♡ K 9 2	♡ A 8 3
	◇ A 8 5 3	◇ K Q 7 2
	♣ K 7 4	♣ A 5 3

WHAT IS THE FIRST THING YOU DO?

Your certain tricks are one spade, two hearts, three diamonds, and two clubs for a total of eight.

WHERE WILL YOUR NINTH TRICK COME FROM?

If the diamond suit divides 3-2 your ninth trick will come from the fourth round of diamonds. The other prospect is the spade finesse. Winning the club lead you play three rounds of diamonds and carefully note they divide 3-2. You now have nine tricks.

Some people think you need a good memory to play the cards well, but this is not the case. You simply have to know what to look for. Here you counted the missing diamonds.

DO YOU FINESSE IN SPADES FOR AN OVERTRICK?

Yes, you should. You have control in every suit so even if it loses no harm will come to you. If a finesse places your contract in jeopardy, you should not take it. Claim your contract instead.

SUIT ESTABLISHMENT

At the same time that you are winning tricks by finessing you can be establishing the small cards in the suit as long suit tricks. All you need is to hold the majority of the suit.

Seven cards may be enough. On a good day this holding will produce four tricks if you tackle it correctly:

Example 4:13 Finessing to set up long suit tricks.

You	Dummy
♡ A Q J 5	♡ 6 4 2

You should lead the two to the queen, then assuming it wins, return to dummy and repeat the finesse by leading the four to the jack. Now you can cash the ace and if the suit divides 3-3 you will have scored four tricks. You are not a favourite to make this many tricks because half the time the finesse will not work and often the suit will not divide 3-3. In fact it is more likely to break 4-2 but if you need four tricks you can but play this way and hope. When you have more cards in the suit your chances are better.

Example 4:14 Finesse with eight.

You	Dummy
♢ A K J 5 3	♢ 6 4 2

To make five tricks play low to the jack in the hope that the queen is with South. Assuming the finesse of the jack works, play off the ace and king and if the suit divides 3-2 (as it figures to do) you have your five tricks.

Incidentally, you may be inclined to play off the ace and king with a holding like the one above, in the hope that the queen will drop. This is wrong. With a total of nine cards in the suit you should play for the queen to drop but with only eight you should finesse.

Sometimes a finesse is just as certain to win as a casino — there is no element of chance. You know it will work. This occurs when a player fails to follow suit marking all the missing cards with his partner:

Example 4:15 Marked finesse.

You	Dummy
♡ K Q 10 8 6 4 2	♡ A 3

You cash the ace and North shows out. This marks South with J 9 7 5 but he will not make a trick. On the second round of the suit you simply take the proven finesse against the jack.

On this hand partner opens one heart, and you finish in three notrumps. Plan the play on the lead of the jack of spades.

Example 4:16 Suit establishment by finesse.

Contract: 3NT	You	Dummy
Lead: ♠ J	♠ 8 3 2	♠ A Q
	♡ 7 3	♡ A 9 8 4 2
	◇ K J 9 8 2	◇ A 7 5
	♣ A 8 2	♣ K 4 3

It is usually better to have the lead coming up to the strong hand rather than through it, as it is here. The spade lead exposing the queen illustrates the point. You are in danger of making just one spade trick, but if partner was declarer it would be worth two. Perhaps partner should have opened one notrump with such washed out hearts. Not to worry, your job is to make nine tricks.

HOW MANY CERTAIN TRICKS DO YOU HAVE?
One spade, one heart, two diamonds, and two clubs. A total of six. Your best chance for extra tricks is in the diamond suit. In the meantime you may as well try the queen of spades in the hope that North has the king. Needless to say, South wins the king of spades and returns another to clear your last control in spades. Now you must tackle diamonds.

HOW DO YOU PLAY THE DIAMONDS?
With eight cards you should finesse against the queen. You cash the ace of diamonds then lead a small one. South plays a low diamond.

DO YOU FINESSE?

The odds favour the finesse so that's what you should do. If it works and the suit divides 3-2, you will make five diamond tricks and your contract.

IMPORTANT POINTS TO REMEMBER
1. Lead towards unsupported honours (up to strength).
2. Only lead honours when they are touching. If there are gaps lead from the opposite hand.
3. Take finesses before you take the certain tricks.
4. Plan ahead so you have the necessary entries.

Chapter 5
THE HOLD-UP PLAY

In this chapter you will learn how you can sometimes take the sting out of an attack on your weakest suit. You will learn how to sever the communication between the enemy hands.

So far, you have been working out ways to establish and promote tricks to add to your total of certain tricks. You have been ruthlessly promoting honours whether they are touching or not and you have been making tricks out of twos and threes. The results have been impressive but you have not yet faced a hostile enemy attack. Sometimes the opponents will threaten you with immediate defeat so you must take defensive action.

When the opponents have the lead they are doing exactly the same things that you are. That is, they are forcing out your top cards to promote winners and they are trying to set up their small cards. You are in danger only if you must lose the lead at a time when you have no *stopper* in the enemy suit. A stopper is another name for a controlling card. It *stops* the enemy suit from being cashed.

In this example the opponents lead spades forcing out your only stopper. Consequently, when you lose to the ace of hearts you are in danger of losing a number of spade tricks.

Example 5:1 The danger of losing control.

You	Dummy
♠ A 3 2	♠ 6 4
♡ J 10 4	♡ K Q 4 3

You cannot stop the spades being established, but you may be able to stop them being cashed. What you should do is refuse to win your trick in spades until the third round. The impact of this can be best illustrated in a diagram.

Example 5:2 How the hold-up play works.

North
♠ K Q J 9 4

You
♠ A 6 2

Dummy
♠ 5 3

South
♠ 10 8 7

If declarer takes the first or second spade with the ace, South will be left with one or two spades which he can use to lead to his partner when he gets the lead. Notice the difference if declarer does not win his ace until the third lead of spades. Now South has no spades which means it is safe to lose the lead to him.

The process of not winning your controlling trick at the first opportunity is called the *hold-up play*. It is used when an opponent is attacking in a suit in which you are in danger of losing control. What you do is withhold your certain trick in the suit until the leader's partner has run out of the suit. Then if the partner wins the lead he cannot continue the attack. You have broken the communications between the defenders.

When the opponents have found your weakest point do not take your certain winner in that suit until the third round.

Example 5:3 Hold-up till third round.

Contract: 3NT
Lead: ♠ K

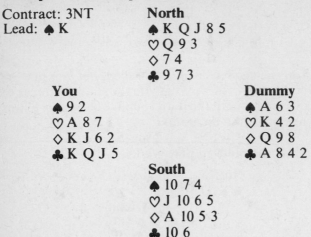

North
♠ K Q J 8 5
♡ Q 9 3
◇ 7 4
♣ 9 7 3

You
♠ 9 2
♡ A 8 7
◇ K J 6 2
♣ K Q J 5

Dummy
♠ A 6 3
♡ K 4 2
◇ Q 9 8
♣ A 8 4 2

South
♠ 10 7 4
♡ J 10 6 5
◇ A 10 5 3
♣ 10 6

North leads the king of spades against your three notrump contract and you naturally begin by counting your certain tricks. You have one spade, two hearts and four clubs for a total of seven. Where can the extra two tricks come from? From diamonds, but what are the opponents threatening to do? After you take your ace of spades they could take the ace of diamonds and four spades which will defeat your contract. What can you do?

You must play on diamonds to make nine tricks so the key is to stop them taking four spade tricks. You do this by holding up the ace of spades until the third round. Be sure you realise why this play succeeds. When South wins the lead with his ace of diamonds he has no further spade to lead to North's established tricks.

Before moving on, two points should be emphasised: firstly, there is no guarantee that South has the ace of diamonds. It is true that if North has the ace you would go down but then there is nothing you can do. By playing properly, at least you make whenever South has the ace. Secondly, do not be afraid to lose the lead even when the opponents have established their suit. If you have to establish tricks then you have to lose the lead. If this involves risk then you must take it because the alternative is automatic failure.

This time you are in three notrumps on the lead of a spade. South takes the ace and returns the jack. Over to you . . .

Example 5:4 Holding up a king.

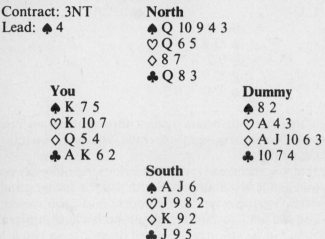

Contract: 3NT
Lead: ♠ 4

North
♠ Q 10 9 4 3
♡ Q 6 5
◇ 8 7
♣ Q 8 3

You
♠ K 7 5
♡ K 10 7
◇ Q 5 4
♣ A K 6 2

Dummy
♠ 8 2
♡ A 4 3
◇ A J 10 6 3
♣ 10 7 4

South
♠ A J 6
♡ J 9 8 2
◇ K 9 2
♣ J 9 5

You now have six certain tricks and the rest will come from diamonds but watch out for the spades.

If you win the king of spades on the second round you will be finished. South will win the king of diamonds when the finesse loses and return his last spade for North to cash the rest of the suit, and you will be one down. What you should do is refuse the second spade and win the third. Now when South wins the king of diamonds he will be out of spades and you will make your contract.

Sometimes you must hold up with two stoppers:

35

Example 5:5 Hold up with two stoppers.

Contract: 3NT
Lead: ♡ Q

North
♠ 9 7 3
♡ Q J 10 8 7 6
♢ A 4
♣ 9 3

You
♠ K 10 4
♡ A 5
♢ J 10 7 6 5
♣ K Q 5

Dummy
♠ A J 6
♡ K 4 3
♢ Q 8 3 2
♣ A 7 4

South
♠ Q 8 5 2
♡ 9 2
♢ K 9
♣ J 10 8 6 2

North leads the queen of hearts against three notrumps. You have two spades, two hearts, and three clubs. The other two must come from diamonds.

Assume that you incorrectly win the ace or king of hearts on the first round and lead a diamond. South will win the king and return a heart, clearing your final stopper. Now you cannot afford to lose the lead to North because he is clutching four winning hearts, but he still has the ace of diamonds so you are sunk.

You cannot succeed if you win the first heart. Look what happens, however, if you duck the opening lead.

Win the second heart lead with the now bare ace, then play a diamond which South will probably win (it is no better for North to win) and note the important difference. South has no more hearts so he must play another suit. Win this and lead a second diamond, quite secure with your king of hearts intact.

In summary, when the opponents have hit your weak point, if you have just one certain trick, take it on the third round, ducking the first two. If you have two certain tricks, duck the first round.

IMPORTANT POINTS TO REMEMBER

1. When the opponents lead your weakest suit do not take your trick until the third round of the suit.
2. When your weak spot is guarded by two stoppers, you should still refuse to win the first round.
3. Do not be afraid to lose the lead even if one suit is unprotected. Take the chance if you have to.

Chapter 6
ENTRIES

In this chapter you will learn the importance of being able to win the lead in the hand of your choice. In particular, you will learn about ducking plays and their uses.

It is one thing to deflect the enemy attack with the hold-up play, it is another to plan your entries. That means being in the right hand at the right time. It is no good working hard to establish extra tricks if you cannot reach them. Nor is it any use if you cannot take a finesse that is working, for want of an entry. Avoiding such pitfalls requires forethought.

Example 6:1 The duck.

You	Dummy
♡ 7 6 4	♡ A K 8 3 2

Imagine you need to make four tricks from this suit and you have no side entry to dummy. How should you play?

What you can make depends on how the outstanding cards lie but they are favoured to divide three in one hand and two in the other. If you play the ace, king, and another, the two small cards will be good but how can you gain entry to cash them? The answer is that you cannot.

What you must do is play low from *both* hands on the first or second round of the suit. This simple expedient will allow you to win the lead in dummy *when the suit is established*. Ducking plays follow the general principle that you should **give away early any tricks that must be lost.**

. Consider this hand:

Example 6:2 A duck and two finesses.

Contract: 3NT
Lead: ♠ 7

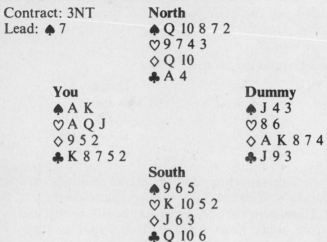

```
                    North
                    ♠ Q 10 8 7 2
                    ♡ 9 7 4 3
                    ◇ Q 10
                    ♣ A 4

You                                Dummy
♠ A K                              ♠ J 4 3
♡ A Q J                            ♡ 8 6
◇ 9 5 2                            ◇ A K 8 7 4
♣ K 8 7 5 2                        ♣ J 9 3

                    South
                    ♠ 9 6 5
                    ♡ K 10 5 2
                    ◇ J 6 3
                    ♣ Q 10 6
```

North leads a low spade against your three notrumps which you win. You only have five certain tricks so there is much to be done. The diamonds will produce two more after you have given one away, assuming the normal 3-2 break, but this is still only seven in total. The other two could come from hearts or clubs. By the time you can make two club tricks, however, the opponents will have taken their spades so you must look to hearts.

To make two extra heart tricks you will have to find the king with South and lead through him twice. You must therefore make good use of dummy's two entries.

You should win the spade and duck a diamond. They will drive out your last spade stopper and now you cross to dummy with a diamond. Next you must take the heart finesse. It is true that you are wide open in spades and that if North has the king of

39

hearts the roof will fall in, but you should take such risks to make your contract. When the queen of hearts wins, you lead your last diamond to dummy. This scoops up the opposition's last diamond so the suit is established. Run the rest of the diamonds, repeat the heart finesse and the contract is yours.

On some hands it is hard to get the lead where you want it. By thinking ahead you can anticipate some of these problems and overcome them. How do you play in three notrumps on the lead of the jack of spades?

Example 6:3 Overtaking an entry crisis.

Contract: 3NT	You	Dummy
Lead: ♠ J	♠ K Q 5	♠ A 6 2
	♡ A J 9 4	♡ 7 3
	◇ K	◇ A J 10 9 8
	♣ A 8 5 3 2	♣ 9 7 4

You have seven certain tricks and the extras could come from diamonds or clubs. If you play on clubs you must lose the lead at least twice. This means the opponents may be able to beat you by attacking your weak heart holding. It is better to play on diamonds but there is an obstacle. Say you win the king of spades, play the king of diamonds and cross to the ace of spades. Now you can cash the ace of diamonds and promote the small cards by giving a trick to the queen, but you have no entry card in dummy.

Can you see a solution to this problem? Try this. Play the king of diamonds and *overtake* with the ace. Now the lead is in dummy so you can play a second round to force out the queen. No difference, apart from one thing; your entry card, the ace of spades is still intact. Later on when the diamonds are established, it can be used as an entry.

If you are very short of entries to one particular hand, be certain to make good use of those you have.

Example 6:4 Making full use of entries.

Contract: 3NT
Lead: ♠ 3

You	Dummy
♠ 9 7 6	♠ A K 4
♡ A Q J	♡ K 6
◇ A Q J 10	◇ 9 7 3
♣ 9 7 3	♣ Q 8 5 4 2

North leads the three of spades against your three notrump contract. You have six top tricks and the rest must come from the diamond suit. To make three extra tricks in diamonds you need to find South with the king and finesse through him. South may have three or even four diamonds so you may have to finesse three times.

When you take a spade trick you must right then and there take a diamond finesse. You will make your contract if South has the king provided you repeat the finesse when you use both of dummy's other entries.

IMPORTANT POINTS TO REMEMBER
1. Work out your entry requirements as part of your planning.
2. Give away unavoidable losers early.
3. Take risks to make your contract, rather than meekly accepting defeat.

Chapter 7
WHICH SUIT
TO ESTABLISH

In this chapter you will learn what to look for when faced with a choice of suits to establish. You will learn to consider the length of the suit, the number of extra tricks it will provide and the time element.

Playing notrumps is a matter of establishing the tricks you need and taking them. While you are promoting and establishing your tricks the opponents are setting up theirs so you must be conscious of the *time* factor. That is, you must take your tricks first.

It is a race and here are three pointers to help speed you up. When deciding which suit to play consider these factors, listed in order of importance:

1. **Play on the suit that will provide the most extra tricks.**The more tricks a suit supplies, the less you need from other quarters.
2. **Play on the suit with the most cards.** The more cards you have in a suit, the more likely it is to behave.
3. **Play on the strongest suit.** The stronger a suit is, the less often you will have to lose the lead.

This example shows how it can be critical to play on the suit that will provide the most tricks.

Example 7:1 Play the suit that provides most tricks.

Contract: 3NT
Lead: ♠ 3

North
♠ Q 9 7 3 2
♡ 6 5
◇ 8 3 2
♣ A 9 4

You
♠ K 6
♡ A Q 3 2
◇ K 10 6 4
♣ Q J 2

Dummy
♠ A 4
♡ K 8 7
◇ Q J 7
♣ K 10 8 7 3

South
♠ J 10 8 5
♡ J 10 9 4
◇ A 9 5
♣ 6 5

Your certain tricks are just five. You can promote extra tricks in either clubs or diamonds but you do not have time to establish both suits. The trouble is that you only have one spade stopper left so when you drive out the first of the minor suit aces they will establish their spades. If you have to lose the lead to the second ace, they will take their spade winners.

Therefore, you can only afford to lose the lead once. This means you must establish nine tricks by losing the lead just once. So the crucial issue is how many tricks each suit will provide.

The diamonds will bring you three tricks, but because of the extra length, the clubs will provide four. Consequently, you must play a club.

Plan your play in three notrumps. The lead is a small diamond.

Example 7:2 Establish the longest suit first.

Contract 3NT	You	Dummy
Lead: ◇ 4	♠ K 6 3	♠ Q 4 2
	♡ K Q 5	♡ J 10 7 3
	◇ A Q 7	◇ K 8 2
	♣ A 4 3 2	♣ K 7 6

You have five certain tricks: three diamonds and two clubs.

WHAT ABOUT THE OTHER FOUR?
The touching heart honours can be promoted into three tricks by driving out the ace, and the spades are always worth a trick. You must first lose the ace in both suits.

DO YOU PLAY HEARTS OR SPADES?
You may think it doesn't matter but it does. Your hearts are longer and stronger so you should play them first. Play the king, the honour from the shorter hand first.

WHY NOT A SPADE?
Your contract would be in danger if one opponent happened to start with five spades to the ace, and the ace of hearts. He would pounce on your spade honour with his ace and return the suit to clear your final stopper.

When you turned your attention to hearts, he would grab his ace and cash his established spades. In all he would take four spade tricks and the ace of hearts to take you one down.

This may not be a big risk but why take any chance if you don't have to? Just play it safe by working on the hearts first.

The time element can prompt you to make a play that you might have otherwise missed.

Example 7:3 The race is on.

Contract: 3NT
Lead: ♠ Q

North
♠ Q J 9 8 6
♡ J 9 5 3
◇ 9 4
♣ K 3

You
♠ K 7
♡ Q 7 4
◇ A K 6 5 2
♣ J 7 5

Dummy
♠ A 3
♡ A 8 6
◇ Q J 7
♣ Q 10 8 6 2

South
♠ 10 5 4 2
♡ K 10 2
◇ 10 8 3
♣ A 9 4

You have two spade tricks, one heart, and five diamonds. You only need one more trick. The clubs can certainly be promoted but the problem is that you have only one spade stopper left. When you force out the first high club they will clear your last spade stopper, and when you lead the second club they will cash three spades to defeat you. You are behind in the race. Can you do anything?

Yes you can. Look at the heart suit. You have one certain trick and you can make another giving you your contract if South has the king. You must lead a heart towards the queen. If North has the king this play will not work but you should try it nevertheless. By playing on clubs you give yourself no chance. At least this line will triumph half the time —whenever South has the king. A 50% chance is better than none.

Think through the play of this hand. The contract is three notrumps and the lead is the queen of hearts.

Example 7:4 Establishing your tricks in time.

Contract: 3NT	You	Dummy
Lead: ♡ Q	♠ A Q J 7	♠ K 9
	♡ K 7	♡ A 5
	◊ J 10 4	◊ Q 9 8 6 3 2
	♣ K Q J 10	♣ 8 3 2

You have six certain tricks so you need three more.

WHERE CAN THE EXTRA TRICKS COME FROM?
You can set up four diamond tricks by losing to the ace and the king, or you can establish three tricks in clubs by losing to the ace.

WHICH OF THESE SUITS SHOULD YOU ESTABLISH?
While the diamond suit will provide more tricks, you only need three tricks and the club suit will provide them. The danger in playing on diamonds is that you have to lose the lead twice and you only have one controlling card left in hearts. This is not enough. You must therefore play on clubs, where you only have to lose the lead once.

HOW WILL YOU PLAY THE SPADE SUIT?
Be careful not to block the suit. You must play the king first and then lead the nine across to the three honours in your hand.

When you are considering which suit will bring you the most tricks, do not count certain tricks in that suit because you have already counted them.

> **PLAY ON THE SUIT THAT
> BRINGS THE MOST EXTRA TRICKS**

Example 7:5 Do not count your tricks twice.

Contract: 3NT
Lead: ♡ Q

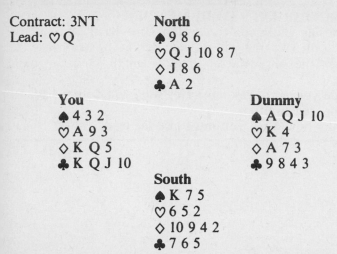

North
♠ 9 8 6
♡ Q J 10 8 7
◇ J 8 6
♣ A 2

You
♠ 4 3 2
♡ A 9 3
◇ K Q 5
♣ K Q J 10

Dummy
♠ A Q J 10
♡ K 4
◇ A 7 3
♣ 9 8 4 3

South
♠ K 7 5
♡ 6 5 2
◇ 10 9 4 2
♣ 7 6 5

North leads the queen of hearts against your three notrumps. You have six certain tricks. It is tempting to play on spades because if the finesse works you will have four tricks. Even when the finesse loses you will still have three tricks in the suit.

Nevertheless, it would be a mistake to play on spades and on the actual layout, it would lead to defeat. South would win the king and return a heart. Now you can take three spades in all, three diamonds and two hearts but when you lead a club, North will hop up with the ace and take his hearts. That would be one down.

The correct play is a club and not a spade. North will take the ace of clubs and clear the hearts just as before but now you have your three diamonds, two hearts, one spade, and three clubs for your contract.

The difference is that you have one certain trick in spades anyway so you only established **two** extra tricks where in clubs you set up **three** extra tricks.

IMPORTANT POINTS TO REMEMBER

When choosing which suit to develop, consider these points:

1. Play on the suit that will provide the most **extra** tricks.
2. Play on the suit with the greatest length, counting both hands.
3. Play on your strongest suit. This way, you do not have to lose the lead so often.
4. Consider how often you must lose the lead.

Chapter 8
THE DANGER HAND

In this chapter you will learn when one defender
becomes the danger hand. You will learn to recognise
the situation and to develop techniques to neutralise
the danger.

The play in notrumps is a race between the declarer and the
defenders to establish and cash their tricks. Consideration of the
opponents' prospects in the race will sometimes influence the suit
you choose to play on, as you have seen.

While we have been mindful of the enemy plans and the time
element in setting up tricks, we have not been concerned with what
each individual opponent is holding. On some hands it can be fatal
for you to lose the lead to one hand but perfectly safe to lose it to
the other. When this is so it is important to recognise the situation
because perhaps something can be done about it.

When one defender has winners but his partner has none, he is said to be dangerous. For example:

Example 8:1 North becomes dangerous.

	You	Dummy
	♡ A 6 4	♡ 5 3 2

North leads the king and you naturally hold up. He continues the queen and South discards. Communications have been broken between the defenders because South has no more of the suit. North is said to be the *danger hand* because he has a number of winners that he is threatening to take, while South is perfectly harmless.

One defender may become dangerous when he threatens to expose your honours to finesse:

Example 8:2 Protecting a secondary honour.

            North
            ◊ Q 10 8 6 2
You   **Dummy**
◊ A J 3   ◊ 5 4
            South
            ◊ K 9 7

North leads the six of diamonds. South plays the king and you win the ace. Winning the ace is your only chance of making a second trick. If you hold up, South will continue the suit and only your ace can make. After you win the ace at trick one your second stopper in the suit is safe, **unless** South can win the lead. South can lead through, allowing North to finesse against your jack. With North on lead, however, your jack is a certain stopper. In this layout, South is said to be the danger hand.

Example 8:3 Keeping the hand with winners off lead.

Contract: 3NT

Lead: ♠ K

You	Dummy
♠ 9 8 7	♠ A 4 2
♡ K 4 2	♡ A 9 6
◇ K J 9 2	◇ A 10 8 3
♣ K Q 6	♣ A 4 2

North leads the king of spades against your three notrumps and you take stock. You have eight certain tricks and the ninth must come from diamonds.

ARE THERE ANY DANGERS?

Yes, you may have to lose the lead to the queen of diamonds to establish your ninth trick and the opponents may take the opportunity to cash four spade winners to beat you by one trick.

IS THERE ANYTHING YOU CAN DO?

To begin with you should hold up the ace of spades. When there is some danger in one particular suit, as here, the hold-up play should be the automatic response. Spades are continued and you win the third round on which South discards a heart.

WHAT NOW?

You can play for the queen of diamonds to drop under the ace or king, or you can finesse through either player.

WHICH LINE DO YOU CHOOSE?

You have nine tricks once you establish the extra diamond so it is only a question of safety. If you lose the lead to North he has two more winning spades but if you lose to South you are safe. He has no spade to lead, thanks to your hold-up play. You should therefore cash the king of diamonds and lead the jack, letting it run if North does not produce the queen. This way your contract is rock solid.

In the last example, North was the danger hand because if he won the lead he had the material to defeat you.

A hand may be dangerous to you if it can lead through your protecting honours, exposing them to a finesse.

Example 8:4 Protect your vulnerable honours.

Contract: 3NT	You	Dummy
Lead: ♠ 5	♠ K J 4	♠ 7 6 2
	♡ A Q J 10	♡ 9 7 3
	◇ Q 7 6	◇ A K 4
	♣ 7 4 2	♣ A Q J 10

In your usual contract, the spade lead from North goes to South's queen and your king.

WHAT DO YOU THINK THE SPADE LAYOUT IS?
If South had the ace he would have played it so it appears that North has some spade suit headed by the ace.

WHAT IS THE DANGER?
Your jack of spades is still protection against the run of the spade suit unless South can win the lead. He would return his partner's spade lead allowing North to scoop up your jack and take the rest of the suit.

WHERE CAN YOUR TRICKS COME FROM?
You have six certain tricks, including the one you have just made. Where can the extra tricks come from? If the heart finesse or the club finesse works you will have nine tricks.

DOES IT MATTER WHICH SUIT YOU TACKLE?
Yes, it certainly does. If you take a club finesse and it fails, your spade weakness will be exposed and you will be defeated on the spot (assuming North started with five spades). If, however, you lead a diamond to dummy and take a heart finesse and North wins the king you can still fall back on the club finesse. Two chances are better than pinning all your hopes on one, so you should play on hearts.

One small point: if the heart finesse loses you should still take the club finesse even though you will be badly defeated if it fails. Always take risks to try and make your contract.

How do you play this three notrump contract on a small spade lead?

Example 8:5 Taking a safety finesse.

Contract: 3NT	**You**	**Dummy**
Lead: ♠ 6	♠ K 8 3	♠ A Q 7
	♡ K 5 4	♡ 7 2
	◇ A 10 8 3	◇ K J 9 6
	♣ A Q 4	♣ K 9 6 2

HOW MANY CERTAIN TRICKS DO YOU HAVE?
Eight: three spades, two diamonds, and three clubs.

WHERE WILL YOUR NINTH TRICK COME FROM?
If you are lucky the club suit will divide 3-3 but that is against the odds. Before playing on clubs you should finesse for the queen of diamonds. Even if this loses you will have nine tricks.

WHO DO YOU PLAY FOR THE QUEEN OF DIAMONDS?
Your consideration is the danger hand! You may be well protected in spades but look at the hearts. If North has the ace sitting over your king and South has the lead you are in danger of losing three, four, or even five heart tricks.

WHAT IS YOUR PLAN?
You should keep South off lead. Play a diamond to the king and lead the jack for a finesse. Even if this loses you are safe because they can only take one heart trick when North has the lead.

Often you will have to develop more than one suit. The order may be critical:
When developing more than one suit, lose the lead to the danger hand early, not later.

53

This hand illustrates the power of the technique:

Example 8:6 Lose to the safe hand last.

Contract: 3NT
Lead: ♠ Q

North
♠ Q J 10 8 7
♡ A 7 3
♢ 4 2
♣ 8 7 6

You
♠ K 9 4
♡ J 10 9
♢ Q J 10 6
♣ K 10 9

Dummy
♠ A 2
♡ K Q 6 4
♢ A 9 7 3
♣ A 4 2

South
♠ 6 5 3
♡ 8 5 2
♢ K 8 5
♣ Q J 5 3

HOW MANY CERTAIN TRICKS DO YOU HAVE?

Five. Two spades, one diamond, and two clubs. What about the extra four? Diamonds will provide two or three more (you have already counted the ace) depending on whether the finesse works. Hearts will bring another two or three depending on whether they divide 3-3 or not.

WHAT DO YOU PLAY AT TRICK ONE?

Spades are your weakest point. You should duck the lead in **both** hands. Sensing he has hit your achilles tendon, North will plug away with spades, forcing you to take the ace.

WHAT DO YOU PLAY NOW?

You have to set up tricks in both hearts and diamonds. Does it matter which you play first? Yes, it does. Either player could win the heart, depending on who has the ace but only South can win the diamond if you take the finesse.

The principle when establishing two suits is to lose the lead to the danger hand first. In this case North is the danger hand so you should play a heart in case he has the ace. After winning the ace of hearts, your last spade control, the king, will be forced out but you are safe. You can take the diamond finesse, knowing that if South has the king, he will not have the two spade winners to defeat you.

This is a difficult hand. To succeed you have to make two good plays. First, you have to duck the spade lead. If you don't, South will have a small spade left to lead to his partner when he takes the king of diamonds. Second, you have to play on hearts ahead of diamonds, otherwise North can win the ace of hearts when his spades have been established.

IMPORTANT POINTS TO REMEMBER
1. When a player establishes tricks in a suit which his partner has run out of, he is the danger hand.
2. When your stoppers may be subject to finesse, the defender who can lead through is the danger hand.
3. When one hand is *dangerous,* play to lose the lead, in the process of developing tricks, to the other player.

SECTION 2

PLAY IN A SUIT CONTRACT

INTRODUCTION

When your partnership has the majority of one particular suit you can enjoy an advantage by calling it trumps. This allows you to step in and take control when you have run out of the suit that is led. This section reveals how you can use the trumps to your advantage.

Trumps are often viewed as a "security blanket", protecting against the danger of the enemy suit. Apart from being a useful hedge, trumps introduce a whole new range of plays that you can put to work alongside your notrump techniques.

First you learn what a trump suit can do for you and how you can neutralise the opposition's holding. Then you learn how to establish extra tricks with trumps without losing the lead. Next you will see how you can use the trump suit to get backwards and forwards and to finish you will learn how to make extra trump tricks.

Chapter 9
DRAWING TRUMPS

In this chapter you will learn why you have a trump
suit and how you should go about playing suit
contracts. You will learn how to draw trumps and
why you should do so.

The principle reason for naming a suit trumps is control. In the
notrump section you were always fortunate enough to have high
cards in all the suits. You used these to stop the opponents
winning long suit tricks. In other words, for control. But what if
you weren't dealt controlling cards in all the suits? Take this
hand:

Example 9:1 Trumps for Control

                    North
                    ♠ 10 9 6
                    ♡ A K Q J 10
                    ◇ 10 7 2
                    ♣ 10 7

West   **East**
♠ Q J 3 2   ♠ A K 8 5
♡ 10 5 3   ♡ 2
◇ K Q 4   ◇ A J 9 8 3
♣ A Q 3   ♣ K 6 5

                    South
                    ♠ 7 4
                    ♡ 9 8 6 4
                    ◇ 6 5
                    ♣ J 9 8 4 2

If West is playing in notrumps he will be disappointed with the
result. He has four spade tricks, five diamond tricks, and three
club tricks for a total of twelve, as soon as he wins the lead. The
trouble is that North leads first. He will lead his top hearts taking
the first five tricks.

While this is going on West can reflect on his problem — lack
of control. Although he had twelve tricks once he won the lead,
he had no control in hearts and was powerless to stop the
opponents running their suit. They took the first five tricks which
left declarer with just eight. Very frustrating for West, but he
could have avoided the problem.

East-West should have called spades (or diamonds) trumps.
Look at the effect this would have had. North cashes the ace of
hearts but if he continues with the king, dummy can step in.
Declarer plays a trump from dummy to win the lead. Now he can
take his twelve tricks.

WHEN TO TACKLE TRUMPS

So you name a trump suit to give you control. The question is, which suit to play when you first win the lead. The usual answer is the trump suit. This is called drawing trumps.

As long as the opponents have trumps, your side-suit winners are in danger. (A side-suit is one of the non-trump suits.) When the opponents run out of your side-suits they will trump in and win tricks with their small trumps. Therefore, you should usually draw all of the opposition's trumps.

DRAW TRUMPS AT THE FIRST CONVENIENT OPPORTUNITY

DRAWING THEIR TRUMPS

Let's put you in the hot seat straight away. You are in four spades from West. North leads the three of hearts.

Example 9:2 Trumping to win the lead

Contract: 4 ♠	**You**	**Dummy**
Lead: ♡ 3	♠ Q J 8 7 3 2	♠ A K 9
	♡ K Q 6	♡ A 5 4
	◇ 7	◇ 8 4 2
	♣ 9 7 3	♣ A 8 6 2

You are certainly in the right contract. Three notrumps would have been hopeless because you lack a diamond stopper.

You win the king of hearts. What now? The reason you called spades trumps was so that you could control the diamonds by trumping in when you could no longer follow suit. While the opponents have trumps they can possibly do the same to your side-suit winners. You can avoid this risk, however, by removing their trumps. Just lead trumps until they have none left. In the hand above there are four trumps missing. Play the ace and king. If both of the opponents follow suit twice, they will have none left. If one player shows out on the second round there is still one outstanding so you will need to draw a third round. Once you draw trumps you are certain to make your contract. You have six trump tricks, three hearts, and the ace of clubs.

If you make the mistake of playing hearts before drawing trumps you will lose your contract whenever one of your opponents is short in hearts. The grateful opponent will make one of his small trumps.

When drawing the trumps you should use all the normal techniques of suit development. How do you go about playing this hand in four spades?

Example 9:3 Drawing trumps with a finesse.

Contract: 4 ♠
Lead: ♡ 2

You	Dummy
♠ J 10 9 8 2	♠ A Q 5 4
♡ 9 8	♡ A 7 4
◇ K Q 5	◇ 7 4 3
♣ Q 5 4	♣ A K 8

North leads the two of hearts. You take the ace; now what? The first thing you should normally do is draw trumps. Do you therefore play the ace of spades?

No! You should lead towards the strength, as usual. Lead a club to the queen and play the jack of spades finessing North for the king.

WHEN TO STOP DRAWING THE TRUMPS

You should normally play enough rounds of trumps to eliminate all the trumps from the defenders' hands.

There is one important exception. When the opponents have just one trump left and it is the best, leave it alone. It will take one trick no matter what you do. You will waste two of your trumps (one from each hand) if you force them to take it.

It is different if there are two trumps outstanding, whether or not they are best. Now you should play an extra round in the hope that they will fall together. In that case you will lose one trick instead of two.

60

This hand shows what can happen to you if you force out the best trump, instead of getting on with establishing your tricks:

Example 9:4 Leaving the Best Trump Outstanding

Contract: 4 ♠   **You**   **Dummy**
Lead: ◇ A

You	Dummy
♠ K 8 3 2	♠ A 7 5 4
♡ J 5 4	♡ K Q 6
◇ 3	◇ 9 6 5
♣ A K Q 8 6	♣ J 4 3

Your bidding continues to impress. You bid to the excellent four spades which requires little more than a reasonable division of the trumps and some careful play.

North cashes the ace of diamonds and optimistically continues with the king but you dash his hopes by trumping in. You play off the ace and king of trumps with both opponents following suit. What do you do now?

There is only one trump outstanding and it is best. Leave it alone!

Play off the clubs throwing the losing diamond away from the dummy. The player with the queen can trump in at any time but everything is under control. After the diamond has been thrown from the dummy you can set up the heart suit by forcing out the ace.

If you had played a third round of trumps you would have been instantly defeated. You would have been out of trumps and there would have been a second losing diamond in dummy. One heart, one trump, and two diamond losers would have been one too many.

IMPORTANT POINTS TO REMEMBER
1. Draw all the opponents' trumps unless there is only one left and it is best.
2. A trump suit gives you control so that you can step in and win the lead.
3. In drawing the trumps use the usual suit management techniques.

Chapter 10
DISCARDING LOSERS

In this chapter you will learn how to count losers and form a plan. You will also learn techniques for discarding losers, including taking a quick discard, discards by finessing, and establishing suits for discards.

The first thing to do when playing notrumps is to count the certain tricks. In a suit contract, it is useful to know how many certain tricks you have, but the number of tricks the opponents are threatening to take is more important. The reason is that in a suit contract there are many ways to eliminate unwanted losers, unlike in notrumps where there is little you can do.

Your first task in a suit contract should be to count your losers. This will help you to answer the critical question of whether it is safe to draw trumps straightaway. If you are facing more losers than you can afford, you must form a plan to avoid defeat. For example, you may be able to *discard* one of the losers on a winner. With AQ3 in dummy and K5 in hand you could play the king followed by the five to the queen. Then on the ace you could discard a loser.

HOW TO COUNT LOSERS

The number of losers depends on the length of the suit and the honours that are held in both your hand and dummy.

Look first at the shortest holding in the suit. It may be a singleton, a doubleton, or three or more. Then check if there are honours to cover these cards.

You	Dummy
♡ 8 6 4	♡ 9 7 3 2

You have three losers.

You	Dummy
◇ J 7 3	◇ 8 5 2

You have three losers.

You	Dummy
♣ 5 4	♣ J 8 3 2

You have two losers.

You	Dummy
♠ A 8 5 3	♠ 6

You have no loser, but you will need three trumps in dummy or discards to take care of the 8-5-3. This should be taken into account in the planning.

You	Dummy
♣ A 6 5	♣ 8 3 2

You have two losers.

You	Dummy
♡ A 8 4	♡ K 6 5

This time you only have one loser.

You	Dummy
♠ A 6 3	♠ K 8

You have no loser because the small card can be trumped in dummy.

Try counting the losers in this hand:

Example 10:1 Drawing trumps — discarding a loser.

Contract: 4 ♡	**You**	**Dummy**
Lead: ♣ K	♠ Q 2	♠ A K 4
	♡ K J 9 8 3 2	♡ A Q 6 4
	◇ 7 6	◇ 8 5
	♣ 9 7 2	♣ A 8 4 3

Start with the trump losers; you have none. You have no spade losers, but you have two in diamonds. Now that they have forced out your ace of clubs, you have two club losers. In all you have four.

FORMING A PLAN
Forming a plan is just as important in suit play as it was in notrumps. It may not be easy but always make the effort. These are the steps you should take:
1. Count your losers.
2. If your contract is not at risk simply draw trumps in the normal way. If you contract is in danger, devise a plan to reduce the losers.
3. Having formed your plan, check whether you can afford to draw trumps immediately.

For practice, apply this procedure to the previous hand. You have four losers, one more than your budget allows. If you lose the lead at this point you will be swiftly defeated so you must form a plan to reduce your losers from four to three **before** you lose the lead.

How can you get rid of one of your losers? The quickest way to unload a loser is to discard it on a winner. In this case, the spade suit will do the job. You have three spade tricks but only two spades in hand. On the third spade trick you can shed one of those irritating losers. You are in good shape, but there is more to think about.

Can you afford to draw trumps first? You should do so unless your attention is urgently needed elsewhere. You must shed your loser before you lose the lead, but trumps can be drawn without giving up the lead. So the answer is yes. Draw trumps, then play the queen of spades (honour from the shorter holding first) followed by a spade to the ace and king on which you can discard one of your losers.

Try the procedure on the same hand without the ace of trumps:

Example 10:2 Taking a fast discard then drawing trumps.

Contract: 3 ♡	**You**	**Dummy**
Lead: ♣ K	♠ Q 2	♠ A K 4
	♡ K J 9 8 3 2	♡ Q 7 6 4
	♢ 7 6	♢ 8 5
	♣ 9 7 2	♣ A 8 4 3

HOW MANY LOSERS DO YOU HAVE?
Two clubs, two diamonds, and the ace of trumps. This is one more than you can afford.

CAN YOU REDUCE YOUR LOSER COUNT?
Yes. The spade suit will provide a parking spot for one loser.

CAN YOU AFFORD TO DRAW TRUMPS?
No! If you lead a trump the opponents will grab their ace and take their four side-suit winners to defeat you.
   You must play spades immediately, starting with the queen. Once a loser has been discarded you can get on with the business of drawing trumps.

On the two examples so far, the winner that you used to discard a loser was ready to cash. It will not always be this easy. Sometimes you will have to establish the necessary tricks for yourself:

Example 10:3 Establishing a discard before drawing trumps.

Contract: 3 ♡	You	Dummy
Lead: ♣ Q	♠ Q 2	♠ K J 4
	♡ K J 9 8 3 2	♡ Q 7 6 4
	◊ 7 6	◊ 8 5
	♣ K 7 2	♣ A 8 4 3

This is a similar problem to hand 10:2, but a different solution is required.

HOW MANY LOSERS DO YOU HAVE?
The two major suit aces, two diamonds, and one club. Five in all, one too many.

CAN YOU DISCARD A LOSER?
Once the spade ace is out of the way you will have an extra winner for a discard. Your plan should be to set up the spade suit for a discard.

CAN YOU AFFORD TO DRAW TRUMPS?
The way to work this out is to follow the play through in your head. If you were to win the club and lead a trump the opponents would take the ace and lead another club. You could plan to extract their trumps and play the queen of spades. This, however, is doomed to fail. They would win the ace of spades and expose the weakness of your scheme. They would simply cash one club and two diamond tricks to defeat you.

WHAT CAN YOU DO?
The trouble is that you do not have **time** to draw the trumps. You have to take the risks associated with leaving small trumps outstanding because your loser problem needs urgent attention. You should win the club and immediately play the queen of spades. They can take their ace and continue clubs, as before, but you are in control. Take the king of clubs and cash your two spades, throwing a loser on the second. Then, having dealt with

the emergency, you can revert to the normal play of drawing trumps.

Sometimes the suit you need to set up for a discard will be missing important honours. Then you must take a finesse or two.
How do you play this hand in six hearts on the lead of the queen of clubs?

Example 10:4 Discarding a loser by finessing.

Contract: 6 ♡	You	Dummy
Lead: ♣ Q	♠ 5 4	♠ A Q J
	♡ K J 8 7 3	♡ A Q 5 4
	◇ J 5 2	◇ K Q 4
	♣ 9 5 4	♣ A K 8

HOW MANY LOSERS DO YOU HAVE?
One spade if South has the king, one diamond, and one club. A total of three.

HOW CAN YOU REDUCE YOUR LOSERS?
You can do nothing about the ace of diamonds, but what about the other two? If North has the king of spades you can take a finesse. Lead a spade from hand and play the queen (or jack) when North plays low. That will take care of the spade loser but what about the club? You can repeat the spade finesse when the queen of spades wins; return to hand with a trump and lead another spade. When North plays low, play the jack. Now cash the ace to discard your club loser. Playing this way you will make your contract when North has the king of spades.

WHAT ABOUT IF SOUTH HAS THE KING OF SPADES?
There is nothing you can do. You will go down.

You should always try to make your contract, even if you end up going down further as a result. This hand is a good example:

Example 10:5 Finessing to shed a loser.

Contract: 7 ◇	**You**	**Dummy**
Lead: ♡ K	♠ A Q 7	♠ 8
	♡ 4 2	♡ A 7
	◇ Q J 6 4 2	◇ A K 9 8 7 5 3
	♣ K 4 2	♣ A Q 6

Your partner got such a pleasant surprise when you opened one diamond that he put you in a sporting seven diamonds. North leads the king of hearts. What do you do?

HOW MANY LOSERS DO YOU HAVE?
Just one heart, but that is one too many.

CAN YOU ELIMINATE THE LOSER?
The only hope is the spade finesse. If you lead a spade from dummy and play the queen from hand, it will win when South has the king. Now the ace of spades will take care of the heart loser. If the spade finesse loses they will cash a heart and defeat you by two tricks.

WHAT SHOULD YOU DO?
Do not have the slightest doubt. Take the spade finesse to try to make your contract.

SAY YOUR CONTRACT IS SIX DIAMONDS . . .
Now the position is very different. Your contract is sure since you only have one loser. By taking the spade finesse you will make an overtrick when it works but you will be defeated when it fails. You should not consider taking a risk for such a small gain as an overtrick. You should simply win the heart lead, draw trumps and concede one heart trick to make your contract.

Notice that in the last example you took the discard in dummy and not your hand as you did in the other examples. This may seem obvious but enough people overlook it to make it worth mentioning. You can trump the loser in dummy but **only** if dummy has trumps.

68

To be a successful declarer in suit contracts you must know how to form an effective plan. As a reminder, here are the planning steps again:

1. Count the losers.
2. If you are safe, draw trumps; if not, work out a plan to rid yourself of the surplus losers.
3. Bearing your plan in mind, check whether you can afford to draw trumps.

Apply the procedure to this hand:

Example 10:6 Taking a fast discard by finesse

Contract: 6 ◇
Lead: ♡ Q

You	Dummy
♠ A Q 4 3	♠ 5
♡ A 8 4	♡ 7 6
◇ J 9 7 5	◇ K Q 8 6 4 3 2
♣ A 2	♣ K 6 4

HOW MANY LOSERS DO YOU HAVE?
One heart and one diamond.

HOW CAN YOU ELIMINATE ONE?
You are obviously stuck with the loss of the ace of trumps but you can do something about the heart loser. You can take a spade finesse, succeeding when South has the king.

CAN YOU AFFORD TO DRAW TRUMPS FIRST?
If you give them the lead they will take their heart winner to defeat you so the answer is no. You must clear the loser first.

WHAT IS YOUR PLAN?
You have to lead a spade from dummy and you only have one quick entry, the king of clubs. What you must do is win the ace of hearts and cross to the king of clubs. Now lead a spade for the finesse. When the queen wins (fingers crossed) you cash the ace and discard the heart loser. Now you are safe to draw trumps.

IMPORTANT POINTS TO REMEMBER

1. Count losers by looking at the length and honours in both your hand and dummy.

2. After counting the losers, work out a plan to discard any excess.

3. Decide if you can afford to draw trumps immediately.

4. Always aim to make your contract even if you must take risks.

Chapter 11
SETTING UP SIDE-SUITS

In this chapter you will learn how to establish long
suit tricks using trumps.

Once the trumps are taken care of, you usually look to side-suits
for extra tricks and discards. Winners are much easier to come
by in suit contracts because of the flexibility you enjoy with a
trump suit. In the previous chapter, you were shown how to
promote tricks to discard losers. In this chapter, you will find out
how to establish long suit tricks using trumps.

A side-suit can be a useful source of tricks. Play this hand in
four spades on the lead of the queen of clubs:

Example 11:1 Drawing trumps and running a side-suit.

Contract: 4 ♠
Lead: ♣ Q

You	Dummy
♠ K Q J 7 4	♠ A 5
♡ A 5	♡ K Q J 7 6
◇ 8 5 2	◇ 7 6 3
♣ A 7 3	♣ 9 8 4

HOW MANY LOSERS DO YOU HAVE?
Three diamonds and two clubs.

WHAT CAN YOU DO ABOUT THEM?
The heart suit in dummy can be used to discard three losers. You follow to the first two rounds, but dummy has three extra winners. On these you can park three of your losers.

HOW DO YOU PLAY AFTER THE ACE OF CLUBS?
You must draw the trumps so your winning hearts do not get trumped.

Keep a careful eye on the fall of the enemy trumps. When you are sure you have drawn them all, play the ace of hearts to unblock, followed by a small heart to dummy's good suit. Playing this way you will make eleven tricks in all.

No doubt you found this hand a piece of cake because your side-suit was already established. Sometimes you will have to work harder. Take a suit like this:

Example 11:2 Trumping out a side-suit.

North
◇ Q 9 3

You	Dummy
◇ 7 5	◇ A K 8 6 4

South
◇ J 10 2

In notrumps, you can play off the ace-king then give away a trick to establish the two small cards in dummy. In a suit contract you have an advantage — you do not have to concede a trick to establish the two small cards. On the third round you can play a trump which allows you to establish the two small cards without losing the lead. Doing this, you will often make contracts that would otherwise fail.

TRUMPING TO ESTABLISH A SUIT
You bid aggressively to four spades. How do you plan to justify your optimistic bidding? North leads the ace of diamonds followed by the king and queen, which you trump.

Example 11:3 Drawing trumps then establishing dummy's suit.

Contract: 4 ♠	You	Dummy
Lead: ◇ A	♠ A K Q J 7 4	♠ 6 5
	♡ A 7	♡ K 8 6 4 3
	◇ J 8	◇ 9 6 5
	♣ 7 6 2	♣ A 4 3

HOW MANY LOSERS DO YOU HAVE?
Two diamonds which you have already lost and two clubs. How can you reduce this number? The heart suit gives you the only hope.

HOW DO YOU PLAN TO USE DUMMY'S HEARTS?
The only way the small hearts can be useful is if the opponents have none left. The way to set up the hearts is to play the ace, the king, followed by a third round trumped in hand. If the six outstanding hearts are divided 3-3 the small hearts will be established and you won't have to lose the lead.

CAN YOU AFFORD TO DRAW TRUMPS FIRST?
Yes, you can, and you must. Draw trumps, set up the hearts and cross to the ace of clubs to cash the established heart winners. In all you will make eleven tricks when hearts are 3-3. If they divide 4-2 your contract will fail.

73

Sometimes it will be necessary to trump more than once to set up a suit. You are in six hearts on the lead of the king of spades. What is your plan?

Example 11:4 Trumping twice to establish a suit.

Contract: 6 ♡	You	Dummy
Lead: ♠ K	♠ A 5 2	♠ 6 4 3
	♡ A K Q J 5 3	♡ 7 4
	◇ 6 3	◇ A K 9 5 4
	♣ 5 2	♣ A K 4

HOW MANY LOSERS DO YOU HAVE?
Two spades — one too many.

WHAT CAN YOU DO?
The only hope is to establish a small diamond.

WHEN DO YOU DRAW TRUMPS?
You will have to clear the trumps if you are going to enjoy a small diamond so you should draw them now. Then what?

Play the ace, king and a third diamond, trumping in hand. On the lead of the third diamond, one of the opponents shows out. His partner is clutching a good diamond but you can deal with it. Cross to dummy with a club and play a fourth diamond. When you trump in hand, dummy's last diamond is established as a long suit trick. The remaining club honour will give you the entry to the dummy to cash it. This allows you to discard one of your losing spades, leaving you with just one loser, so your contract makes exactly.

A side-suit does not have to be strong in honours to be useful. All you need is length.

Plan the play in four hearts. North leads the king of spades which holds, then he plays a diamond.

Example 11:5 Establishing a weak side-suit.

Contract: 4 ♡	**You**	**Dummy**
Lead: ♠ K, ◊ 8	♠ 9	♠ Q 8 6 5 4 3
	♡ K Q J 8 7 5 3	♡ A 4
	◊ J 7 6	◊ A 5 3
	♣ 7 2	♣ A 6

HOW MANY LOSERS DO YOU HAVE?
One spade, two diamonds, and one club. A total of four.

HOW CAN YOU REDUCE THIS TO THREE?
The most realistic chance of making this contract is to set up the spade suit. The opponents only have four more spades since they played two on the first trick.

HOW DO YOU ESTABLISH THE SPADES?
You should win the diamond lead with the ace and trump a spade. Assuming both opponents follow, there will only be two spades outstanding. (Remember the opening lead was a spade.) Now play to the ace of hearts and trump another spade. With luck the last two spades will fall together leaving your three remaining spades good. Now all you have to do is draw the remaining trumps and lead to the ace of clubs to take the three established spade tricks. In all, you will make eleven tricks — three spades, six hearts and the minor suit aces.

What, you might wonder, if the spades do not divide 3-3? Don't ask awkward questions!

It is possible to establish an even weaker side-suit. Any five card suit can be established provided there are sufficient entries and the breaks are favourable. This hand illustrates the power of a long suit. Look at how dummy's miserable spade suit is brought to life:

Example 11:6 Establishing a weak suit by careful use of entries.

Contract: 4 ♡
Lead: ♠ A

You	Dummy
♠ 6	♠ 7 5 4 3 2
♡ K Q J 8 7 3	♡ A 5
◊ 8 7 4	◊ A K 5
♣ 8 4 3	♣ A 9 7

North leads the ace of spades followed by the king, which you trump.

HOW MANY LOSERS DO YOU HAVE?
One spade, one diamond, and two clubs. A total of four.

HOW CAN YOU REDUCE YOUR LOSERS?
The only hope is to establish a spade trick. You can do this if the suit divides 4-3. You must trump out three rounds to leave the small spade best.

HOW DO YOU GO ABOUT THIS?
Draw trumps making sure you don't discard a spade and cross to the ace of diamonds to trump a spade. Both opponents follow suit so there is only one spade left outstanding. Cross to another winner and trump out the last spade. Then triumphantly return to dummy to cash your established winner.

The suit you are establishing does not have to be in dummy. In the following hand you bid soundly to four spades. North leads the queen of hearts which you optimistically cover with the king and South takes the ace. A heart is returned which you trump. How do you plan the play?

Example 11:7 Establishing a side-suit in hand.

Contract: 4 ♠	You	Dummy
Lead: ♡ Q	♠ K Q J 7 3	♠ A 8 6 4
	♡ 5	♡ K 8 6
	◇ A K 9 5 2	◇ 8 7
	♣ 8 7	♣ Q 6 4 3

HOW MANY LOSERS DO YOU HAVE?

One heart, two clubs, and no diamond losers — as long as dummy has trumps. You play two rounds of trumps on which both opponents follow suit.

WHAT DO YOU DO NOW?

All the trumps have been drawn so establish your second suit, the diamonds. Play the ace, king, and a third round trumping in dummy. On this South discards a club. North still has the best diamond but that is no problem.

Trump a heart to get the lead in your hand and play a fourth round of diamonds trumping in dummy. Now your small diamond is established. When you take your last trump in hand you can cash your carefully established tenth trick.

It is worth noting that if you had failed to count the enemy trumps and incorrectly played a third round you would have been defeated. Dummy would have been left with only one trump so you could not have trumped both your diamond losers.

FINESSING TO ESTABLISH SIDE-SUITS

All the side-suits you have worked on so far have called for taking established tricks and trumping out the opposition's winners. Sometimes, you will have to do more.

On this hand you are playing in five diamonds. North leads a low heart, South plays the king.

Example 11:8 Finessing to establish a side-suit, after trumps.

Contract: 5 ◇ **You**   **Dummy**
Lead: ♡ 2   ♠ 7 4   ♠ A Q 6 5 3
                ♡ A 7 3   ♡ 9 8 6
                ◇ A K Q 8 3 2   ◇ 9 7 6
                ♣ 9 8   ♣ A 4

HOW MANY LOSERS DO YOU HAVE?
Two hearts, one club, and perhaps one spade depending on who
holds the king.

WHAT CAN YOU DO TO REDUCE THE LOSERS?
You can establish the spade suit.

HOW DO YOU PLAY?
You must hope that North has the king of spades. If it is with
South you are doomed. South would take his king and the
defenders could cash two heart tricks to defeat you. Win the
heart lead and start by drawing trumps.
    Now play a spade. Assuming the finesse of the queen wins,
cash the ace and play a third round of the suit, trumping in hand.
Your good luck continues when both opponents follow suit so
your two small spades in dummy are winners and the contract is
yours.

IMPORTANT POINTS TO REMEMBER
1. It is possible to establish long suit tricks in any suit that is five
   cards or longer.
2. Trump losers to establish your side-suits, whether they are in
   dummy or your hand.
3. Take finesses and lead up to strength in your side-suits.
4. Count the outstanding cards in your side-suits so you know
   when your small cards have become winners.

Chapter 12
ENTRIES IN SUIT CONTRACTS

In this chapter you will learn how to plan your entries. You will also find out how entries can help you overcome bad breaks in your side-suits.

An entry card is one that will win the trick when the lead comes from the hand opposite. An entry allows you to transfer the lead from one hand to another.

Working out your entry needs is an important part of planning. You must think ahead to where you will want the lead and make sure you have the necessary entries. Then plan the sequence of play. **In general, retain the entry cards in the hand that contains the suit you intend to establish:**

Example 12:1 Retaining an entry to dummy.

Contract: 7 ◇ **You** **Dummy**
Lead: ♣ 3

♠ A 9   ♠ 8 7 3
♡ 7 6   ♡ A K 5 3 2
◇ A K Q J 9 6 ◇ 5 4
♣ A 8 4   ♣ K 7 5

HOW MANY LOSERS DO YOU HAVE?
One club and one spade.

WHAT CAN YOU DO ABOUT IT?
The only hope is to establish the hearts, but first you should draw trumps.

HOW CAN YOU SET UP THE HEARTS?
You will need to be lucky. You should play off the ace, king and trump a third round. If the six outstanding hearts are divided 3-3, you will be successful in setting up the two small hearts. Your contract will make, provided you have an entry card to the dummy.

WHAT ABOUT ENTRIES?
It is no use establishing the hearts unless you can enter the dummy to cash them.

HOW DO YOU PLAN TO DO THIS?
The king of clubs is the only possible entry to dummy, outside the heart suit. What you must do at trick one is win the club lead in hand with the ace, thereby preserving the vital entry to dummy. Now, after the two heart winners have been established, you can cross to dummy with the king of clubs.

It is often difficult for the inexperienced declarer to anticipate in which hand he will need to have entry cards. The idea is to **keep entry cards in the hand where you plan to establish tricks.**

The trump suit is usually rich in entries.

Example 12:2 Trumps for entries.

You	Dummy
♡ A Q J 5 3	♡ K 10

If you need entries to dummy for some purpose this suit will provide two — the king and the ten. If you start by drawing trumps, however, you will destroy the entries to dummy in the suit.

Retaining entry cards is the most common reason for delaying the drawing of trumps.

Example 12:3 Establishing a suit before drawing trumps.

Contract: 4♠
Lead: 4 ◇

You	Dummy
♠ A K Q 8 3	♠ J 6 5
♡ Q 7	♡ K J 10 5
◇ A K 2	◇ 9 6 5
♣ A 4 2	♣ J 9 6

HOW MANY LOSERS DO YOU HAVE?
One heart, one diamond, and two clubs. You must reduce your losers by one.

HOW CAN YOU DO THIS?
The heart suit is the obvious answer. You can establish the heart suit by first leading the queen and forcing out the ace of hearts.

ANY PROBLEMS IN ESTABLISHING THE HEARTS?
It is easy to set up the hearts, but what about an entry to dummy so you can cash them?

WHAT WILL BE YOUR ENTRY CARD?
The only possible entry outside the heart suit is in trumps. If you follow the normal advice of drawing trumps straight away you will kill the trump entry.

Instead, play the queen of hearts, and a second round if they play low, to force them to take the ace. Now win their return and play the ace-king of trumps. If both opponents follow there will only be one trump outstanding. Play a low trump to the jack, to both pick up the last survivor and transfer the lead to dummy with the two winning hearts.

The same type of play may be required when you have all the top cards in your side suit, but it is blocked:

Example 12:4 Unblocking a side suit before trumps.

Contract: 4 ♠	You	Dummy
Lead: ♣ K	♠ K Q 9 5 3	♠ A 7 4
	♡ A K	♡ Q J 10 7
	◇ A 8 3	◇ 9 7 6
	♣ 6 3 2	♣ 9 8 5

The defence gets off to a good start by taking the first three club tricks, then switches to a diamond. How do you go about taking the rest?

HOW MANY LOSERS DO YOU HAVE?
Three clubs and two diamonds.

HOW CAN YOU SHED TWO OF YOUR LOSERS?
The heart suit should be the object of your attention. You have four heart winners if you can play off the ace and king, then enter dummy to play off the other two tricks. They will take care of your two losing diamonds, but you will have to be careful that they do not get trumped. To avoid this, you will have to draw the trumps first.

WHAT IS YOUR PLAN?

You must win the ace of diamonds, unblock the hearts and draw trumps ending in dummy. This is how. Play off the ace-king of hearts and cash the king-queen of spades. Assuming both opponents follow suit, there is only one trump outstanding. Play a trump to the ace in dummy which will draw the last trump and leave you where you want to be. Now cash your two heart winners.

You may be apprehensive about playing off the ace, king of hearts before drawing trumps. There is some chance that one might be trumped but unless you play this way you have no hope of making your contract. You should always try to make your contract even if it means taking risks, especially ones like this.

A similar situation will often exist when you are trumping out dummy's suit.

Example 12:5 Establishing a suit by trumping — using trumps for entry.

Contract: 4 ♠   **You**   **Dummy**
Lead: ◊ 8   ♠ A K 9 8 2   ♠ Q 5 3
                  ♡ K 7   ♡ A 9 6 5 3
                  ◊ A 6 2   ◊ 7 5 4
                  ♣ 8 4 3   ♣ 7 5

This is another ambitious contract and to be successful you will need a bit of luck.

HOW MANY LOSERS DO YOU HAVE?
Two diamond and two club losers. While you only have two club losers you also have the third club in hand to worry about. You are going to need two extra tricks for discards. That means you will need the heart suit. For this, the six outstanding hearts must divide 3-3. If they are 4-2 you can only ever set up one trick even if you have the entries.

IF HEARTS DIVIDE 3-3 ARE THERE ANY PROBLEMS?
Yes, there is an entry problem. If you draw trumps then establish the hearts by trumping the third round you will create two winners. But they will be stranded in dummy.

CAN YOU MAKE BETTER USE OF DUMMY'S ENTRIES?
The only possible entry to dummy outside the heart suit is in trumps so you should set up the hearts **before** drawing the trumps. After winning the ace of diamonds at trick one, play the king followed by the ace and a third heart, trumping in hand.

When the hearts fall 3-3, play the ace, king and a third spade to the queen. This should draw all the outstanding trumps and you will be in dummy to take the two vital heart tricks and make your contract.

OVERCOMING BAD BREAKS

By postponing drawing the trumps you may be able to overcome a bad break in your side-suit:

Example 12:6 Overcoming a bad break in a side-suit.

Contract: 4 ♠	You	Dummy
Lead: ♣ A	♠ K Q J 10 8 7	♠ A 9
	♡ 7 6	♡ A K 8 5 4
	◇ 8 5 2	◇ A 4 3
	♣ 7 3	♣ 9 8 2

North leads the ace, king and a third club against your four spades.

HOW MANY LOSERS DO YOU HAVE?

Two diamonds and two clubs, so you need one extra trick. The only chance for this trick is in hearts.

AFTER TRUMPING THE CLUB, WHAT DO YOU LEAD?

You could draw trumps and play on hearts, trumping the third round. This would set up the two small cards if the enemy hearts divide 3-3. If the hearts divide 4-2, however, you would be finished. You would have only one entry to dummy — the ace of diamonds — and you would need two: one to trump out the last heart and another to reach the winner you create.

HOW CAN YOU SUCCEED WHEN THE HEARTS DIVIDE 4-2?

What you have to do is use the trump entry to dummy. This means you must postpone drawing trumps. After trumping the club, play the ace, king and a third heart and trump. If the hearts divide 3-3 you have no further problem. Simply draw trumps and take your eleven tricks (four hearts, six spades and the ace of diamonds).

85

If someone shows out on the third round of hearts, you will be pleased you did not draw trumps. The time has come to use the carefully preserved entry to the dummy; play to the ace of spades. Then lead a fourth round of hearts to clear the last obstacle. Now you are home. Draw the trumps and lead over to the ace of diamonds in dummy to take the hard-earned heart winner.

While you should always form a plan before you play to trick one, do not doggedly stick to it no matter what happens. The way your critical suits divide may give you reason to change tack.

Example 12:7 Overcoming a bad trump break.

Contract: 4♠	You	Dummy
Lead: ◇ Q	♠ A 6 5 2	♠ K Q 8 7
	♡ 10 6 3	♡ K Q J 5 2
	◇ K 9 7	◇ A 8 5
	♣ J 6 3	♣ 5

HOW MANY LOSERS DO YOU HAVE?
You are looking good. There are just three: one diamond, one club and one heart. You expect the trumps to divide three-two which will allow you to set up the heart suit and throw away your losing diamond.

DO YOU DRAW TRUMPS?
Yes, you should plan to draw the trumps, then set up the hearts.

WHERE DO YOU WIN THE OPENING LEAD?
You should win in hand, following the general principle of retaining the entry cards in the hand that contains the suit to be established. Then play trumps. Lead to the king of spades and back to the ace. Both opponents followed to the first trump lead but North showed out on the second.

WHAT DO YOU DO NOW?
If you play even one more round of trumps, you will be in dire

straits. This is what will happen. You need heart tricks so you must knock out the ace. If the defender with the ace of hearts also has the best trump he will teach you a lasting lesson. He will draw your last two trumps and hit you with an avalanche of clubs.

Instead of playing a third round of trumps, you should establish the heart suit, so that when they take the ace you still have trumps headed by the queen. They can play on clubs but you can trump in and play off your heart winners. The opponent with the four trumps can trump in but you still have control. This is the position after the second lead of trumps:

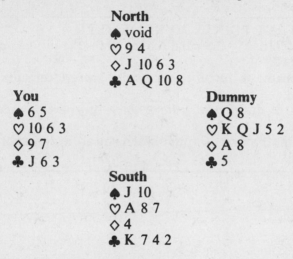

North
♠ void
♡ 9 4
◇ J 10 6 3
♣ A Q 10 8

You
♠ 6 5
♡ 10 6 3
◇ 9 7
♣ J 6 3

Dummy
♠ Q 8
♡ K Q J 5 2
◇ A 8
♣ 5

South
♠ J 10
♡ A 8 7
◇ 4
♣ K 7 4 2

When you play the ten of hearts, South can take the ace and play a club. North will win the queen and say he plays the ace (nothing is better), you trump in dummy and now you cash the queen of spades. This is safe because you no longer have to lose the lead to set up tricks. Play the hearts from the top and South will eventually trump in while you throw your club loser away. When South leads a winning club, you trump and cross to the ace of diamonds to take the rest of the heart winners. You make your contract exactly, losing one trump, one club, and the ace of hearts.

This last example was complex. It illustrates two points. First, it is important to retain entries to the hand with the suit that is being developed. Second, you should abandon drawing trumps when your control is threatened.

The same type of play is called for when you find yourself in a flimsy trump suit. When you only have seven trumps between the two hands your control is threatened so you should usually postpone the drawing of trumps until you have established the tricks you need.

IMPORTANT POINTS TO REMEMBER
1. Retain entries to the hand that contains the suit you plan to establish.
2. Be prepared to modify your plan if the critical suits break badly.
3. Delay the drawing of trumps when they will be needed as entries.
4. Delay the drawing of trumps when you are in danger of losing control.

Chapter 13
MAKING EXTRA TRICKS
FROM TRUMPS

> In this chapter you will learn how you can use
> dummy's trumps to make extra tricks and reduce the
> total of losers. You will also learn why it is a mistake
> to trump in the long hand without a good reason.

One of the neatest and most appealing ways to make extra tricks
is to trump losers in the *short hand*. That is, the hand with fewer
trumps. This is usually dummy. Take a trump suit like this:

Example 13:1 Tricks for free.

You	Dummy
♡A K Q 6 2	♡J 9 3

You can always play out the suit and make five tricks. You could
also trump some card with the two and make four other tricks
for the same total of five. Contrast this with trumping a loser
with the three. That is one trick and your five winners in hand are
still intact. In this way you will make six tricks. If you could also
trump a loser with the nine you would make a total of seven
trump tricks.

The opportunity for trumping losers in dummy does not occur on every hand. **What you need is a suit where dummy holds less cards than you.** This example shows how you can take advantage of such a situation:

Example 13:2 Trumping in the short hand

Contract: 7 ♠	**You**	**Dummy**
Lead: ♣ 10	♠ A K Q J 6	♠ 7 5 4
	♡ Q J 6 2	♡ A K 7 3
	◇ A J 6	◇ 8
	♣ 7	♣ A J 6 3 2

Here you are in another threadbare grand slam. You have two diamond losers which need attention. There are no winners on which they can be discarded, so another plan is called for.

WHAT CAN YOU DO WITH THE DIAMOND LOSERS? The winning play is to make extra trump tricks by using dummy's trumps. You started with two diamond losers in hand but you can take advantage of dummy's singleton diamond, **so long as dummy has trumps.**

This is how you do it. Win the club lead. Then, before you draw trumps, play the ace of diamonds and trump a diamond in dummy. Enter hand with the queen of hearts to trump your last diamond in dummy. Now lead dummy's last trump and draw the outstanding trumps. Your two diamond losers have disappeared.

Be sure you know what happened. You made two extra tricks with dummy's small trumps. In effect, you made tricks with little trumps that would otherwise have fallen helplessly under your boss trumps.

Note, you could not afford to draw trumps first. That would have removed dummy's trumps which were your means of extra tricks. When you plan to trump losers in dummy you will usually have to postpone the drawing of trumps.

DO NOT TRUMP IN THE LONG HAND

Let us have another look at the earlier diagram.

You   **Dummy**
♠ A K Q 6 2   ♠ J 9 3

As previously noted, trumping losers with dummy's trumps adds to your total number of tricks, while trumping losers with your own holding does not.

In addition, **trumping losers with the long trump holding can waste your trumps and cause you to lose control.** Take this earlier hand where you played seven spades:

Example 13:3 Don't waste trumps.

Contract: 7 ♠
Lead: ♣ 10

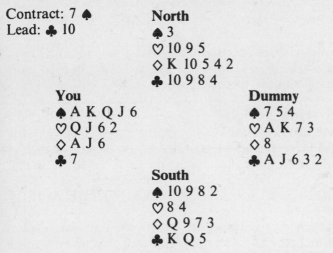

North
♠ 3
♡ 10 9 5
◇ K 10 5 4 2
♣ 10 9 8 4

You
♠ A K Q J 6
♡ Q J 6 2
◇ A J 6
♣ 7

Dummy
♠ 7 5 4
♡ A K 7 3
◇ 8
♣ A J 6 3 2

South
♠ 10 9 8 2
♡ 8 4
◇ Q 9 7 3
♣ K Q 5

North led the ten of clubs, which you took with the ace. The winning play was to trump your two diamond losers in dummy. Imagine you made the poor play of trumping a club in your own hand at trick two. You would be left with the same length in spades as South. Then, if you made the mistake of trumping a second club, you would be defeated. You would be down to three trumps and South's four card holding would take a trick.

WHEN TO DRAW TRUMPS
When you have to trump losers in the short hand, you will have to give close consideration to whether you can afford to draw the trumps first. Normally, you cannot:

Example 13:4 Postponing drawing trumps.

Contract: 3 ♡	**You**	**Dummy**
Lead: ♠ J	♠ A K 3	♠ 6 5
	♡ K Q J 7 6 2	♡ 8 3
	◊ 8 7	◊ A J 9 4
	♣ 6 2	♣ 8 7 5 4 3

Your contract is three hearts and the lead is a spade. You have four losers: one heart, one diamond and two clubs, but you must do something with the three of spades.

WHAT IS YOUR PLAN?
You cannot hope to establish the clubs because you lack the entries, and there are no extra winners. To have a chance of making this contract you must trump the small spade in dummy.

WHAT DO YOU PLAY AFTER WINNING THE ACE OF SPADES?
You should not play a trump. If you do, the opposition could win the ace and play a second round which would take dummy's last trump. Instead, you must immediately eliminate your spade loser. Play the king of spades and trump the third round in dummy. This reduces your five losers to four so you make your contract.

You need a trump in dummy for every loser you plan to trump. If drawing trumps would strip dummy of the trumps needed to cover losers, then postpone drawing trumps until you have taken care of the losers. But if you can afford to draw trumps anyway, then do so. For example, you are in seven spades on this hand. North leads a club. Your bidding has style, does your card-play?

Example 13:5 Drawing trumps early.

Contract: 7 ♠	**You**	**Dummy**
Lead: ♣ 4	♠ A K Q J 7	♠ 10 6 5 2
	♡ A K 8 5	♡ 6 3
	◇ 4	◇ A K 8 5
	♣ A Q 7	♣ K 5 3

HOW MANY LOSERS DO YOU HAVE?
You have two heart losers. This is a grand slam so you must do something about both.

WHAT IS YOUR PLAN?
One can be discarded on a diamond and the other can be trumped in dummy.

SHOULD YOU DRAW TRUMPS?
Usually you will have to trump losers in dummy before drawing trumps otherwise dummy will run out. Here, however, you only have to use one trump in dummy. Since it will still be there after the opposition's trumps have been removed, you can afford to draw trumps straight away. This avoids the risk of a defender trumping a heart.

Always draw trumps if you can afford to do so. Only put it off when you have a particular reason.

On the last hand you were best to put off trumping losers in dummy, prefering to draw trumps. There is another time when trumping losers should not be your top priority:

Example 13:6 The importance of establishing suits.

Contract: 4 ♠
Lead: ♣ 8

You	Dummy
♠ A Q J 6 4	♠ K 10 9
♡ 9 7 6 5	♡ 4 2
◇ 7	◇ K Q J 10 6 3
♣ A 7 3	♣ K 9

HOW MANY LOSERS DO YOU HAVE?
Three: two hearts, and one diamond. Everything should be fine because the diamond suit will be a parking place for your two losing hearts and the small club. You could also trump a loser or two in dummy.

WHERE DO YOU WIN THE CLUB LEAD?
Since you plan to establish dummy's diamonds, retain the entry card to dummy, take the first trick with the ace of clubs in hand.

DO YOU TRUMP THE CLUB LOSER IN DUMMY?
This would be a fatal mistake. You are going to establish the diamonds and you will need the king of clubs and the trumps for entries. To trump a club would destroy the vital entries.

DO YOU DRAW TRUMPS?
No. You need the third trump to be an entry to dummy so you must first establish the diamonds. Lead your diamond which is taken by the ace. A club is returned knocking out the entry.

WHAT DO YOU PLAY NOW?
You are in the clear. Draw trumps ending in dummy and cash the winning diamonds.

CREATING A SHORTAGE IN DUMMY
In order to trump losers in dummy there has to be a suit in which dummy has fewer cards than declarer. In some cases both hands may start out with equal length, but you can create the necessary shortage by discarding one of dummy's cards:

Example 13:7 Discarding to create a shortage

Contract: 4 ♠
Lead: ♣ A, ♡ Q

You	Dummy
♠ A Q J 8 5	♠ K 10 2
♡ A 5 3	♡ 7 4 2
◇ A J 8	◇ K Q
♣ 8 5	♣ 9 6 4 3 2

North wins the first trick with the ace of clubs, against your contract of four spades. He then turns his attention to your other weakness, he plays a heart.

HOW MANY LOSERS DO YOU HAVE?
Two hearts and two clubs; the familiar situation of one too many.

WHAT CAN YOU DO ABOUT IT?
You can probably set up one or two winners in the club suit by trumping out the remaining cards, but there is a problem. You first have to clear your last club. Then the opposition would take the opportunity to cash their two heart winners, putting you down.

CAN YOU SEE THE SOLUTION?
There are no extra winners in dummy, but there is one in hand! What you should do is play three rounds of diamonds discarding a small heart from dummy. The position looks like this:

You	Dummy
♠ A Q J 8 5	♠ K 10 2
♡ 5 3	♡ 7
◇ void	◇ void
♣ 8	♣ 9 6 4 3

Now you can do something about one of those heart losers. Play a heart before drawing trumps. When you get the lead play your last heart and trump it in dummy.

It is worth noting that when your trumps are strong like this, you should trump the heart loser with the **ten** of spades to avoid any possibility of being overtrumped.

IMPORTANT POINTS TO REMEMBER
1. Trumping losers in the short hand adds to your tricks.
2. Trumping losers in the long hand does not add to your tricks and weakens your control.
3. When you have extra winners in hand, consider throwing losers from dummy, to create a shortage.
4. When planning to trump losers in dummy, you will usually have to postpone the drawing of trumps.
5. Only draw trumps immediately if you will be left with enough trumps in dummy for all the losers you plan to trump.

SECTION 3

DEFENCE

INTRODUCTION

Defence will bring you some of your highest moments in bridge, and some of your lowest. To succeed in defence you and your partner have to work in together. For this reason, defending is the most challenging aspect of bridge.

When you play the hands you can see your total assets but when you are defending you can only see the dummy and your hand. You are often left to work out what your partner holds by inference. There is unlimited opportunity to use creative imagination in defence.

A lot of contracts can be beaten with accurate defence and so you must learn the techniques of good defence if you are to be a successful player. This section sets out the basic techniques of defence. It is by no means a complete list of defensive play, but knowing these techniques will put you ahead of the average player.

Suit and notrump defence are considered together. The principles are usually the same. Differences are noted where they occur.

Chapter 14
THE OPENING LEAD

In this chapter you will learn which suit to lead
against both notrump and suit contracts, taking the
bidding into account. You will also learn which card
to select once you have decided on a suit.

The job of the defenders is little different to that of the declarer.
They are trying to set up their long suits by driving out declarer's
stoppers, just as declarer is doing. It is usually a race which is won
by the first side to assemble its quota of tricks.

There are two notable differences between declaring and
defending. Firstly, the defenders cannot see each other's cards.
This makes defence more difficult than playing the hand.
Secondly, the defenders make the opening lead. This means they
have an advantage in the race to establish tricks. Making the best
use of this opportunity is important to good defence.

WHICH SUIT TO LEAD

If you were declarer, you would normally establish the suit in which your side holds the most cards. As a defender you should do the same. Take a look at this hand. You are on lead against three notrumps. In which suit do you think your partnership has the most cards?

Example 14:1 Leading without clues from the bidding.

> **Your hand**
> ♠ A 6 5
> ♡ Q 9 6 4 3
> ◇ K 7 4 3
> ♣ 5

You do not know for sure which is your partnership's longest suit. It depends on your partner's holding in each suit. It could be in any one of the four suits, but the chances are it will be in your own longest suit. In general, therefore, **you should lead your longest suit.** In this case you should lead a heart.

Lacking other information, a heart lead has the best chance of striking your main strength, but there are usually other factors to consider such as the bidding and the quality of the suit.

THE INFLUENCE OF THE BIDDING

The bidding often tells you where the opponents are strong. It obviously makes good sense to take this information into account:

Example 14:2 Indications from the bidding.

> **Your hand**
> ♠ A 7 4 3 2
> ♡ J 5
> ◇ K 8 5 3
> ♣ 7 3

Which suit do you lead against three notrumps after this bidding?

1 ♣	1 ♠
1NT	3NT

Normally the spade suit would offer the best outlook, but that has changed. One of the opponents has bid spades, so your partner is likely to be very short in spades. The bidding has made it clear that spades are not your best fit so you should try something else. In this case you should lead a diamond.

You should hardly ever lead a suit that has been bid by the opposition. **Always prefer an unbid suit:**

Example 14:3 The enemy bids three suits.

West's hand
♠ 6 4
♡ K Q 10 7
♢ Q 6 3 2
♣ 9 6 4

North	East	South	West
1 ♡	pass	1 ♠	pass
2 ♣	pass	3NT	All pass

Without the bidding you might have tried a heart lead because the suit is strong but the opening bid has changed that. Three suits have been bid so you should strongly favour the lead of the fourth suit, diamonds in this case.

WHEN PARTNER BIDS
Never lose sight of what you are trying to do. You are aiming to play on the suit where you have the best fit. This does not mean that **you** must always have length. Partner has gone to the trouble of bidding because he has a good suit that he would like you to lead. Do what he says, it's his fault if it doesn't work.

All the same, you have to use some judgement. For example, there is a difference between a one club opening and an overcall of one spade. The one club opener could be based on a poor suit but an overcall should always be a robust collection. Take this hand:

Example 14:4 Leading partner's suit.

West's hand
♠ Q J 10 9 5
♡ 8 6
◇ J 7 4 3
♣ 4 3

North	East	South	West
1 ◇	1 ♡	2NT	pass
3NT	All pass		

What do you lead? You may be tempted to try your spades, they are quite strong after all. Nevertheless, this is wrong. Your partner's bid suit is probably better so lead a heart. Even if it does not work he will be pleased you took notice of his bid.

Another small point in favour of leading partner's suit is to do with entries. Not only must a suit be established but that defender must win the lead so the suit can be cashed. This takes entries. For this reason, it is usually hopeless to lead a long suit from an otherwise weak hand. If partner has the strength to bid he will usually have enough entries to establish and cash his suit.

> **IF A SUIT IS GOOD ENOUGH TO BID, IT IS GOOD ENOUGH TO LEAD**

WITH SUITS OF EQUAL LENGTH

Lead the stronger suit:

Example 14:5 Choosing between two four card suits.

West's hand
♠ K J 9 5
♡ 6 5
♢ Q 7 3 2
♣ J 7 3

North	East	South	West
		1NT	pass
3NT	pass	pass	pass

What do you lead? There is no indication from the bidding. No suits have been bid. Normally you would lead your longest suit but you have two four card suits. For a diamond lead to be successful partner will need to have two honours, or at least the ace. For a spade lead to work all he needs is one honour, either the ace or queen. You should therefore lead a spade.

> ### WITH SUITS OF EQUAL LENGTH, LEAD THE STRONGER

WITH A SEQUENCE

A sequence of three honours makes a very attractive lead. For example, a suit headed by K-Q-J or Q-J-10. The reason is that sequence leads relentlessly promote tricks for the defence even when partner has nothing. A lead from a broken sequence say K J 8 7 4 is made in the hope that partner will have the queen or ace. When he doesn't you give away a cheap trick.

Example 14:6 One suit contains a sequence.

West's hand
♠ K J 8 6
♡ Q J 10 9
♢ 6 4 3
♣ 4 2

They bid 1NT:3NT. What do you lead?

Both your four card suits are quite strong. You should choose a heart because you have a sequence. With a sequence you should lead the top card, in this case the queen of hearts.

For the spade lead to work you need to find partner with a spade honour to fill the gaps. No such luck is needed with the heart lead. It will set up tricks in due course no matter what partner has.

Some honour holdings are considered to be a sequence even though there are gaps. When you hold a suit headed by K-Q-10, Q-J-9, or J-10-8, it is considered to be as good as a sequence. You should favour leading these holdings as you would a touching sequence. Once again you should lead the top honour.

SUIT CONTRACTS

The ideas mentioned so far apply equally against suit contracts and notrumps. There are three situations that are peculiar to suit contracts: short suit leads, trump leads, and the importance of not leading suits that are headed by an ace.

It is never advisable to lead a low card in a suit that contains the ace. If you must lead that suit lead the ace, but generally, prefer to lead another suit altogether.

The reason is that you cannot expect to take many tricks before declarer starts trumping. By not playing the suit you wait for partner to lead **towards** your strength, and you do not risk giving declarer a cheap trick.

While you shun suits that are headed by the ace alone, you should fall in love with suits topped with the ace-king. The ace lead is highly desirable when it is backed by the king.

SHORT SUIT LEADS

Against a suit contract, a singleton (occasionally a doubleton) can be a good lead. The idea is that partner will win the lead before your trumps have been drawn and lead the suit back for you to trump:

Example 14:7 The singleton lead.

West's hand
♠ 7 5 2
♡ J 9 6 4 3
♢ Q 7 4 3
♣ 7

North	East	South	West
1 ♢	pass	1 ♠	pass
2 ♠	pass	4 ♠	All pass

What do you lead? The prospects for beating this contract are bleak. The diamond lead is unattractive because they have bid the suit and the hearts are very weak. The best chance is to lead your singleton club. Partner could have the ace in which case he can lead the suit back for you to trump. Alternatively, he may win the lead in trumps before all your trumps are drawn for the same result.

The layout you are hoping for is something like this:

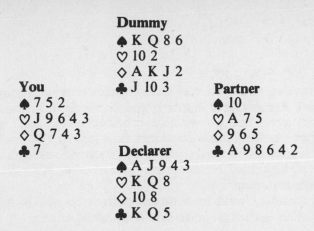

Dummy
♠ K Q 8 6
♡ 10 2
◇ A K J 2
♣ J 10 3

You
♠ 7 5 2
♡ J 9 6 4 3
◇ Q 7 4 3
♣ 7

Partner
♠ 10
♡ A 7 5
◇ 9 6 5
♣ A 9 8 6 4 2

Declarer
♠ A J 9 4 3
♡ K Q 8
◇ 10 8
♣ K Q 5

Partner will win the club and return the suit for you to trump. Noting the futility of leading a diamond, you should lead a heart. Partner will take the ace and finish off a satisfying defence by leading a third round of clubs, which you will trump.

It is worth pointing out that only an original club lead will defeat this contract. On any other lead declarer will make eleven tricks.

WHEN TO LEAD TRUMPS
Think back to the play of the hand in a trump contract. You often had to postpone the drawing of trumps for one reason or another. If declarer wants to delay the drawing of trumps the best move from the defenders is to draw them.

When you sense that declarer is about to trump losers in dummy you can strike back with a trump lead:

Example 14:8 The killing trump lead.

Your hand.
♠ J 9 6
♡ A Q 10 6
◇ 8 7 5
♣ K 6 5

They bid   1 ♡   1NT
          2 ◊   pass

WHAT DO YOU LEAD?

Before making your lead, give some thought to what is going on. What will dummy have in hearts and diamonds? To pass two diamonds rather than give preference to two hearts is a sure sign of dummy's holding more diamonds than hearts. You are likely to see a singleton heart in dummy. Now, what is declarer going to do with all his hearts? He has at least five after all. He is going to trump them in dummy.

You, therefore, must immediately destroy his plan by leading trumps. This is the sort of layout you should expect:

Dummy
♠ K 8 2
♡ 7
◊ K J 4 2
♣ J 9 8 7 3

You
♠ J 9 6
♡ A Q 10 6
◊ 8 7 5
♣ K 6 5

Partner
♠ Q 10 4 3
♡ 9 5 4
◊ A 6
♣ Q 10 4 2

Declarer
♠ A 7 5
♡ K J 8 3 2
◊ Q 10 9 3
♣ A

On your trump lead, partner will win the ace and play a second round. When you win a heart you can play a third round of trumps to leave declarer with just one lonely trump in each hand. He will wind up one trick short.

On any other lead he would be left with at least two trumps in dummy. Thus he could trump two hearts, and make the contract.

Another good time to lead trumps is when nothing else appeals. There is a saying "when in doubt lead trumps" which is not a bad idea:

Example 14:9 The passive trump lead.

West's hand
♠ 7 5 3
♡ A 6 4
♢ Q 5 4 2
♣ J 8 5

North	East	South	West
1 ♣	pass	1 ♠	pass
1NT	pass	3 ♢	pass
3 ♠	pass	4 ♠	All pass

You could try the unbid suit, hearts, but it is better to lead a trump. A word of warning: **only lead a trump when you hold two or three small trumps.** With more, less, or an honour, prefer to lead another suit.

There is another point about the heart lead. Against a suit contract you should never lead a small card in a suit that contains the ace. If you choose to lead that suit lead the ace, but prefer to lead another suit altogether.

WHICH CARD TO LEAD
1. From a Sequence
With a sequence such as K-Q-J, Q-J-10, or J-10-9, or a near sequence such as K-Q-10, Q-J-9, or J-10-8, lead the top card.

2. From a Long Suit
With four cards or more in a suit that does not contain a sequence lead the **fourth** highest card. From K J 9 6 4 lead the six, the fourth card down. Why so? It helps partner to work out how many cards you hold in the suit. For example, if you lead the two you cannot have a five card suit. With the example above you would play the four on the next round unless you had to play an honour. This would tell partner you started with a five card suit.

3. From Three Cards
When leading a three card suit, lead low if you have an honour (the ten or higher) and the top card if you do not. With two honours in sequence lead the top card. K Q 5 lead the king, Q J 6 lead the queen, J 10 2 lead the jack.

4. From a Doubleton
Always lead the top card, even if it is an honour. This is yet another example of playing the honour from the shorter hand first, preventing the suit from blocking.

5. From Ace-King
In a suit contract, when you are leading a suit headed by the ace and king, always lead the ace, not a small card. Against a notrump contract you should make your normal fourth highest lead.

These rules apply to the opening lead. Later leads follow the same pattern but not at the expense of common sense. You should judge each case on its merits.

IMPORTANT POINTS TO REMEMBER
1. Lead your partner's suit.
2. Avoid leading suits bid by the opposition.
3. Lead the top of a sequence.
4. Lead the fourth highest of your longest suit.
5. With equal length suits lead the stronger.
6. Lead trumps when you expect declarer will be trumping losers in dummy, or if nothing else appeals.
7. Against suit contracts, avoid leading suits that contain the ace.

Chapter 15
THIRD HAND PLAY

In this chapter you will learn which card to play when
your partner leads; whether the lead is an honour or a
spot card; whether dummy's holding in the suit is
weak or strong. Also included is how to show partner
you have an honour in the suit he leads.

While the opening lead may be the single most important play by
the defenders, the other plays also matter. It is one thing for
partner to strike the winning lead, it is another for you to ram
home the advantage.

The partner of the leader to each trick is called *third hand*
because he is the third player to the trick. He has to be alert to the
lead, take dummy into account, then choose his card with care.

There are rules to guide third hand and they are set out in this
chapter. You have to know what they are but you should not
follow them blindly. There is no escaping the need to think.

This is always the case in bridge. There are no hard and fast rules; all get broken sometimes. This makes the game hard to master. While this may be frustrating for the inexperienced player it also accounts for its universal appeal.

The defenders are out to do the same thing as declarer; that is, to establish tricks and cash them. It should therefore be no surprise that the defenders use the same techniques as the declarer. They lead **towards** their high honours, take finesses, establish long suit tricks and so on, without the help of being able to see each other's hands.

The lead is generally a low card, in keeping with the principle that you should lead towards your high honours. This gives partner, third hand, the chance to play high or low, depending on what second hand does.

In general, if the lead was a low card, third hand plays his highest card. The major complication is when dummy has an honour that third hand can beat. If the lead was an honour the correct play is more obvious.

DUMMY DOES NOT HAVE AN HONOUR

Example 15:1 Third hand high.

Dummy
♡ 8 6 <u>4</u>

Partner	**You**
♡ 5 led	♡ Q 9 2

On partner's lead of the five, dummy plays the four, what do you play? Some players are reluctant to "sacrifice" the queen and so play the nine in the hope that they can make the queen later. This is wrong. Third hand should play high — the queen.

This could work in two ways: the queen will win the trick if partner has the ace-king, or the play of the queen may promote winners for partner. Take this layout:

Dummy
♡ 8 6 4

Partner
♡ K J 7 5

You
♡ Q 9 2

Declarer
♡ A 10 3

If you play the nine, declarer will make two tricks in the suit. If you play the queen, you will force out the ace and promote the king-jack in partner's hand into winners.

THIRD HAND CANNOT BEAT DUMMY'S HONOUR

The situation is the same when dummy has an honour that third hand cannot beat. Third hand plays high unless dummy's honour is played.

Example 15:2 Dummy has higher honour.

Dummy
♡ K 6 <u>4</u>

Partner
♡ 3 led

You
♡ Q 9 7

If dummy plays a low card, you simply play as though dummy did not have the honour. In other words, you play the queen.

If the king is played from dummy, there is no point in playing the queen, so play a small card.

FOLLOWING SUIT WITH TOUCHING HONOURS

When third hand is playing from touching honours, the lowest honour should be played. (The same applies to second and fourth hand). This is the opposite to what you would play if you were leading.

In the following example, if East were on lead he would play the king, but in following suit he should play the queen.

Example 15:3 Lowest of touching honours.

                    Dummy
                    ♠ 6 <u>4</u>
Partner   **You**
♠ 3 led   ♠ K Q 5

Third hand plays high, but with touching honours you should play the lowest, in this case the queen. With K Q J you should play the jack.

DUMMY HAS AN HONOUR THIRD HAND CAN BEAT

The plan should be to use your honour when dummy's is played. In this example it is fairly obvious to hold back the ace until the king has been played:

Example 15:4 Sitting over dummy.

                    Dummy
                    ♡ K 7 <u>6</u>
Partner   **You**
♡ 3 led   ♡ A Q J

Dummy plays low on partner's lead. It would not be smart to play your highest card, the ace. You should play your jack (lowest of touching honours) to win the trick. You should then lead another suit and wait for the lead to come through the king again, allowing you to make the ace and queen. What you did was take a finesse in defence.

This was easy because you held all the important cards. Usually there will be gaps, even so, you should still wait for dummy's honour to be played.

Example 15:5 Finessing against dummy.

                    Dummy
                    ♠ K 7 <u>6</u>
Partner   **You**
♠ 3 led   ♠ A J 10

Partner leads the three and dummy plays low. What should you play? If partner holds the queen your ten will win the trick. Then you can exit with some other suit and wait for another spade to be played through the king. But what if declarer has the queen?

Dummy
♠ K 7 6

Partner
♠ 9 8 5 3

You
♠ A J 10

Declarer
♠ Q 4 2

It is still best for you to play the ten. Declarer will take the queen, but the next two tricks will go to your ace-jack, which are hovering over dummy's king-seven. If you play the ace you will kill any hope of a second trick in the suit. The king and queen will win the second and third tricks.

In general, keep dummy's honour guarded. Play your next highest card rather than release your covering honour.

This card may not win the trick, but later on you can make sure that dummy's honour is smothered.

Example 15:6 Finessing against dummy.

Dummy
◊ Q 7 2

Partner
◊ J 9 5 3

You
◊ K 10 6

Declarer
◊ A 8 4

Partner leads the three and the two is played from dummy. What should you play? If you play the king declarer wins the ace and has a second trick with the queen.

If you hold back the king to take care of the queen, declarer will only take one trick. Your ten forces out declarer's ace. Later, partner will lead the jack since the jack-nine are now *touching,* and the queen is trapped. Your side takes the next two tricks.

It is also possible that partner could hold A J 5 3 in example 15:6. In this case the finesse of the ten would hold the trick, whereas the play of the king would allow the queen to win the third round of the suit.

Example 15:7 Finessing against dummy's jack.

Dummy
♡ J 8 <u>5</u>

Partner   **You**
♡ 2 led   ♡ K 10 6

Partner leads the two, the five is played from dummy. Once again, you should play the ten. Use the king to cover the jack.

Dummy
♠ J 6 3 <u>2</u>

Partner   **You**
♠ 4 led   ♠ K 9 5

A low card is played from dummy. As usual sit over dummy's honour. Play the nine.

When your second best card is too small to have any effect, you should play the top honour anyway. **The rule is to play the second best if it is the nine or better, otherwise play the honour.**

Example 15:8 Not finessing against dummy.

Dummy
♣ Q 6 <u>5</u>

Partner   **You**
♣ 3 led   ♣ K 7 2

In this case play the king, even though the queen has not been played. Only play the next card down if it is the nine or better.

When an honour is led, third hand should still finesse against dummy's honour:

Example 15:9 Honour leads.

               Dummy
               ♣ K 8 <u>5</u>
Partner   **You**
♣ J led   ♣ A 7 3

You should play low. Declarer will win the queen which he is known to have (partner's lead denies holding that card), but on the next round you have the king surrounded. This will be the position:

               Dummy
               ♣ K 8
Partner   **You**
♣ 10 9 4   ♣ A 3
               Declarer
               ♣ 6 2

Example 15:10 Time to give it a go.
Which card do you play with each of these five holdings?

               Dummy
               ♡ Q 7 <u>4</u>
Partner   **You**
♡ 3 led   a. ♡ K 10 2
                               b. ♡ A J 5
                               c. ♡ J 10 6
                               d. ♡ K 8 2
                               e. ♡ K 9 5 2

SOLUTIONS:
a. The ten. When the queen is played, cover with the king.
b. The jack. Finesse against dummy's queen.
c. The ten. Follow suit with the lowest of touching honours.
d. The king. Only finesse against the dummy if you hold the nine or better.
e. The nine. Finesse with the nine or better.

UNBLOCKING BY THIRD HAND
Remember how as declarer you played the honour from the shorter hand first? This was to avoid *blocking* the suit. The same need arises in defence but it is harder to recognise. Imagine this position:

Example 15:11 Unblocking the king.

Dummy
♡ A 7 3

Partner
♡ Q led

You
♡ K 8

Dummy plays the ace, what should you play? To get this right you must work out what your partner holds. The queen lead shows a suit headed by the Q-J-10 or Q-J-9. Either way, your king is just a nuisance. Partner will have something like Q J 10 x x, leaving declarer with x x x.

If you play the eight, **your king will block the suit.** That is, the second round will be won with your king, but you cannot continue the suit because that is your last card. Then partner may never get the chance to take his J 10 x which are all good. The correct play is to unblock your king. That is, you should play it at trick one. Yes, that's right, under the ace. Then when your side wins the lead you can take all your tricks in the suit.

When partner leads an honour, play a touching honour immediately if it is doubleton.

Here are some more examples:

Example 15:12 Unblocking the queen.

$\qquad\qquad$ **Dummy**
$\qquad\qquad$ ♡ <u>K</u> 7

Partner $\qquad\qquad\qquad\qquad$ **You**
♡ J led $\qquad\qquad\qquad\qquad\qquad$ ♡ Q 3

The king is played from dummy. You should unblock the queen.

Example 15:13 Unblocking whether dummy plays high or low.

$\qquad\qquad$ **Dummy**
$\qquad\qquad$ ◇ A 5 <u>3</u>

Partner $\qquad\qquad\qquad\qquad$ **You**
◇ J led $\qquad\qquad\qquad\qquad\qquad$ ◇ Q 9

Partner has clearly led from J-10-8 to some number. Whether the ace is played or not you should contribute the queen.

Example 15:14 Unblocking the king.

$\qquad\qquad$ **Dummy**
$\qquad\qquad$ ♠ 8 <u>5</u>

Partner $\qquad\qquad\qquad\qquad$ **You**
♠ Q led $\qquad\qquad\qquad\qquad\qquad$ ♠ K 3

You should play the king on your partner's queen.

THE HONOUR SIGNAL

As you have just seen, when an honour is led and third hand has a touching honour that is doubleton, the honour should be played to *unblock* the suit. What should third hand do when it has a touching honour that is not doubleton?

Example 15:15 Signalling an honour.

Dummy
♠ <u>A</u> 7 3

Partner
♠ Q led

You
♠ K 9 2

Dummy's ace is played on the queen. There is no need to unblock the king because it is not doubleton but which small card do you play? What you should do is *signal* partner as to whether you hold an honour in the suit. This is done by the size of the spot card played. A low spot card says you do not have an honour in the suit, a high spot card says you do. This information helps your partner to judge whether to continue the suit or not.

When partner leads an honour and you hold a touching honour: play the honour if you have only two cards in the suit; play your highest spot card if you have three or more. Without a touching honour play your lowest spot card.

Example 15:16 Partner leads an honour, what do you play?
The card played from dummy is underlined.

1.

Dummy
♣ <u>A</u> 6

Partner
♣ J led

You
a. ♣ Q 9 3
b. ♣ K Q 9 3
c. ♣ 7 4 2
d. ♣ K 8 5 3
e. ♣ 9 7 5 2

2.

Dummy
♡ 8 5 <u>4</u>

Partner
♡ K led

You
a. ♡ J 9
b. ♡ A 3
c. ♡ 9 7 3 2
d. ♡ J 6 2
e. ♡ A 9 6 2

118

SOLUTIONS:
1. **a.** Nine, to signal the queen.
   b. Nine, to signal the honours.
   c. Two, share the bad news.
   d. Eight, signal your honour.
   e. Two, discourage.

2. **a.** Jack, unblock the touching honour.
   b. Ace, once again unblock the touching honour.
   c. Two, show the weak holding.
   d. Six, trying to look like a nine.
   e. Nine, come again.

You should be aware that it is not always possible to signal the honour with a high spot and the lack of the honour with a low spot because you may not be dealt the equipment. For example, partner leads the king and you hold the 10-9-8 in the suit. How can you discourage? All you can do is play the eight and hope partner can recognise your problem. On the second round of the suit it will become clear when you play a higher card — the nine — thereby showing that you did not have an honour. A similar problem exists when partner leads an honour and you hold, for example, K 3 2. The three does not look like a high spot card.

So far, the signalling positions have all begun with the lead of an honour. This does not have to be so. When partner leads low and dummy wins the trick, third hand is freed of the need to complete for the trick. This is a good opportunity to give the honour signal:

Example 15:17 Signalling after a spot card lead.

                   Dummy
                   ♡ K̲ 7 4
   Partner   **You**
   ♡ 3 led   ♡ Q 8 2

Dummy wins the king. You should play the eight. If you held 9 8 2, you would play the two.

DOUBLETON SIGNAL

Third hand plays against suit contracts are similar to those in notrumps. The only significant different is that third hand may be able to trump a later round of the suit. Take this situation:

Example 15:18 Signalling for a ruff.

<pre>
                    Dummy
                   ♣ Q J 8 7
      Partner   You
      ♣ A K 6 2   ♣ 9 3
                    Declarer
                   ♣ 10 5 4
</pre>

Partner leads the ace against a suit contract. He would love to know if you have just two in the suit; if so he can continue with the king, then give you a ruff. This defence would not work if you have three and declarer has the doubleton. Partner does not have to guess.

What you should do against a suit contract is play the high card first when you hold a doubleton, otherwise you should play your smallest. In the position above, partner sees your nine and knows to continue with the king and a small one. If, however, you play the three at trick one, partner would know to turn his attention elsewhere.

IMPORTANT POINTS TO REMEMBER

1. With small cards in dummy, third hand plays high.
2. When partner leads an honour, or dummy plays an honour that third hand cannot beat, third hand should signal when holding an honour in the suit.
3. The signal is high to encourage, low to discourage. This is used to show an honour or in a suit contract is may also show a doubleton with an interest in trumping.
4. When the lead is an honour and third hand has a doubleton honour, it should be played to unblock.
5. When dummy has an honour that third hand can beat, he should only play his honour if dummy's is played or if his next highest card is smaller than a nine.

Chapter 16
SECOND HAND PLAY

> **In this chapter you will learn what to play when the player on your right leads.**

When you are second to play to the trick you should generally play low because your partner will be last to play. By doing this, you waste nothing since partner can play high or low according to what third hand does.

Example 16:1 Second hand plays low.

Dummy
♡ Q 9 <u>4</u>

Partner   **You**
♡ K 8 3   ♡ A 10 5 2

Declarer
♡ J 7 6

The four is played from dummy. If you play low your side will take three tricks, but if you play the ace or the ten you will only take two. Suppose you play the ace; declarer can establish one trick with Q 9 opposite J 7. If you play the ten, declarer covers with the jack and your partner wins the king. The queen-nine, which are left in dummy, are worth one trick because the ten, jack and king have been played. If you play low, however, you will take three tricks. Declarer will play the jack which your partner will win with the king. Now you have the ace-ten sitting over the queen-nine in dummy, so declarer will take no trick in the suit. What happened?

WHY SECOND HAND PLAYS LOW

When the opponents lead, your side plays last to the trick. This gives you the advantage of playing high or low according to what the opposition plays. In this case, if declarer plays the seven, partner will win the eight; if declarer plays the jack, your partner has the final say with the king. Nothing is wasted.

How different it is if you smash down your ace. Declarer can safely play low and use the queen and jack later to establish a trick.

The principle is no different if declarer has the king instead of partner:

Example 16:2 Capture an honour with an honour.

Dummy
◇ Q 9 <u>4</u>

Partner
◇ J 8 3

You
◇ A 10 5 2

Declarer
◇ K 7 2

By playing low, second hand can wait around to take an honour with him, thereby assisting the promotion process.

On the lead of the four, if you play the ace, declarer will play low and take the next two tricks with the king and queen. If you play low, as you should, declarer's king will win the trick, but that is all he will take. Your ace-ten sit over the queen, with the jack in partner's hand.

The idea is to use your honours to stifle the opposition's honours. By taking their honours with you, you help to promote the lower cards in both your hand and partner's. In the last example, when you played low, declarer had to play his king to avoid the lurking jack and then your ace-ten sat over the queen-nine. When you take the queen with the ace, partner's jack is suddenly best.

If you fly with the ace you fail to take an honour with you and so the jack does not win a trick. There is an old saying that may help: queens were meant to take jacks, kings to take queens, and aces to take kings.

You should play low even when it is tempting to do otherwise:

Example 16:3 Making declarer's life difficult.

                     Dummy
                     ♣ K Q 6 4
You   Partner
♣ A J 5   ♣ 10 9 2
                     Declarer
                     ♣ 8 7 <u>3</u>

On the lead of the three you may see no point in ducking, and simply hop in with the ace, but you shouldn't. It is true that you will only take one trick but if you play low you oblige declarer to lead this suit from his hand a second time to set up his tricks. This could burn up a vital entry. Playing the ace removes the need for declarer to return to hand. There are other reasons to play low.

Example 16:4 Giving declarer a guess.

                     Dummy
                     ♠ K J 8
You   Partner
♠ A 6 4 2   ♠ Q 10 7 3
                     Declarer
                     ♠ 9 <u>5</u>

Declarer, in a suit contract, plays the five from hand. His problem could be to avoid two losers in this suit. If you wrongly rise with the ace he cannot misguess because his king is good. If you play low he could well finesse the jack in the hope that you have the queen. Partner would win the queen and your ace is yet to come.

WHEN SECOND HAND PLAYS HIGH

Needless to say, there is more to second hand play than mindlessly reaching for your lowest card. The following examples illustrate situations where second hand should play high. They fall into three categories:
1. When an honour is led.
2. When second hand has a sequence of three or more honours.
3. When common sense suggests it.

When an honour is led you should **cover an honour with an honour.** The idea is to take two of theirs for one of yours. This helps to promote your side's lower cards. Some players are reluctant to accept that they should "sacrifice" their honours in this way, so here is some evidence. This example is not challenging:

Example 16:5 Cover the queen with relish.

Dummy
♡ <u>Q</u> 6 5

Partner　　　　　　　　**You**
♡ 8 3 2　　　　　　　♡ K J 10

Declarer
♡ A 9 7 4

The queen is led from dummy, what do you play? You should cover with the king to promote your jack-ten. If partner has the ace you will take all three tricks, if declarer has the ace you will take two. If you fail to cover, declarer will take two tricks when he has the ace.

COVER AN HONOUR WITH AN HONOUR

The following position is basically the same although it may not look it from East's point of view.

Example 16:6 Promoting partner's secondary honours.

	Dummy	
	♡ Q 6 5	
Partner		**You**
♡ J 10 3		♡ K 8 2
	Declarer	
	♡ A 9 7 4	

When the queen is led, it is less appealing to cover with your king. Nevertheless, you should do so. Last time you covered to promote your jack-ten, this time you cover to promote partner's jack-ten. Okay, so you don't know partner has them, but the point is that you hope he does. At least, you hope he has some useful honour — the jack or the ten.

Example 16:7 Promoting a lowly ten.

	Dummy	
	♣ Q 6 5	
Partner		**You**
♣ 10 4 3		♣ K 8 2
	Declarer	
	♣ A J 9 7	

When you cover the queen with the king, you promote partner's ten so that it can win the third round. If you played low the queen would win. Then declarer could avoid any loser in the suit by finessing against your king. All right, you might say, but what if partner has nothing?

In that case your king is doomed no matter what you do. It is also right to cover when partner has the ace.

Example 16:8 Killing the queen.

                    Dummy
                    ◇ Q 6 5
Partner   **You**
◇ A 10 3   ◇ K 8 2
                    Declarer
                    ◇ J 9 7 4

If you play low on the queen, partner's ace will win the trick but now you can only make your king. Declarer will play a low card from dummy towards his jack and can restrict you to just one more trick, for a total of two. If you cover the queen with the king your partner is still good for two tricks with his ace-ten sitting over the jack-nine.

Having made the case for covering an honour with an honour, one exception should be noted. When the hand leading has two honours, you should not cover the first, instead you should cover the second. The position will usually arise when dummy has the two honours because you cannot be sure what declarer holds:

Example 16:9 Cover the last honour.

                    Dummy
                    ♡ J 10 5
Partner   **You**
♡ Q 8 6   ♡ K 9 4
                    Declarer
                    ♡ A 7 3 2

When the jack is led from dummy you should play low because the jack is not the only honour. The jack will run to the queen and now you have the ten surrounded with your king-nine. If the ten is led you cover to ensure a second trick in the suit. If you covered the first honour, the jack, you would restrict your side to just one trick. The ace would take the king and a low card would be played towards dummy. Your side would only take one trick.

   You should also decline to cover an honour when you have great length in the suit without promotable honours.

Example 16:10 Not covering with weak length.

> **Dummy**
> ◇ J 8 6 4
>
> > **You**
> > ◇ K 7 5 3 2

When the jack is led from dummy you should not cover. The reason to cover is to promote tricks but what can your partner have? Probably a singleton, so play low. That way your king will live on to menace the dummy and you will avoid the embarrassment of crashing the singleton queen in partner's hand, if he happens to have it.

The point of second hand playing low is to give partner a chance to win the trick cheaply. There is no point in this if you are very strong in the suit. Play high if you have three honours in sequence.

Example 16:11 Second hand high with a sequence.

> > **Dummy**
> > ♡ 8 5 4
>
> **Partner**   **You**
> ♡ 7 3 2   ♡ K Q J 9
>
> > **Declarer**
> > ♡ A 10 6

A low card is played from dummy. There is a danger that in playing low declarer will win a cheap trick with the ten. Your holding is so strong you do not have to take this chance; play an honour — the jack — you always follow suit with the lowest card of a sequence.

Example 16:12 Second hand high with a sequence.

                    Dummy
                    ♠ A K 9
You   **Partner**
♠ Q J 10 4   ♠ 5 3 2
                    Declarer
                    ♠ 8 7 <u>6</u>

On the lead of the six you should rise with the ten because you
have three honours in sequence. Otherwise declarer can score a
cheap trick with the nine. Some players confuse the previous
layout with this:

Example 16:13 Save your secondary honours.

                    Dummy
                    ◊ K 8 3
You   **Partner**
◊ A J 2   ◊ 9 7 4
                    Declarer
                    ◊ Q 10 6 <u>5</u>

On the lead of the five, it would be wrong to play the ace; it is
equally wrong to play the jack, a play that some people make to
"force out the king." Declarer had to play the king anyway or
lose to partner's nine so all you would do is waste the jack. With
the jack gone, declarer avoids a second loser in the suit.

Common sense will convince you to play *second hand high* on
occasions:

Example 16:14 Asleep at the wheel.

                    Dummy
                    ♣ J 10 9
                      —
Partner   **You**
♣ 5 3 2   ♣ A K Q 7
                    Declarer
                    ♣ 8 6 4

Unless you have nodded off, it is clear to win the lead of the jack with an honour, preferably the queen. There is clearly no advantage in playing low.

You should also grab the trick as second player when you have the contract beaten for sure. There is no sense in playing low with an ace if that is the setting trick and there is some chance it will vanish if you duck. For example, you might play low with the ace and find to your chagrin that declarer has the king and the rest of the tricks.

Example 16:15 Going in with an honour.

Dummy

♡ Q 2

You

♡ A K 9 5

Declarer

♡ 6 led

In a suit contract, declarer plays towards the queen in dummy. What do you do? If you play low declarer will win the queen and you will only take one trick. If you rise with your honours on the first two rounds you will take two.

IMPORTANT POINTS TO REMEMBER

1. Second hand normally plays low *except in the following situations:*

2. When dummy leads an honour, cover unless there is a touching honour in dummy.

3. Do not cover when your partner is likely to be very short in the suit and your holding is weak.

4. Second hand should play an honour when it has a sequence of three or more honours.

5. Second hand should play high when it is clear that to do otherwise would cost.

Chapter 17
DISCARDS

In this chapter you will learn what to play when you
cannot follow suit.

In discarding, you have two aims: firstly, to hold on to your
winners and secondly, to signal your strength. Keeping winners
and throwing losers does not sound like an awesome challenge
but sometimes it is not obvious which is which.

The safest discard is from a long suit. Fifth and sixth cards are
seldom needed so they make attractive discards. Once these have
gone it is more difficult.

KEEPING PROTECTION
For your honours to carry their full weight, they must be
accompanied by small cards. This is called keeping protection.
The number you must keep depends on the honour:

Example 17:1 Keeping protection for the jack.

> **Dummy**
> ◇ K Q 6 3

Partner
◇ 10 4

You
◇ J 9 7 2

> **Declarer**
> ◇ A 8 5

Holding the jack, you need three small cards as protection. Declarer can play the ace, king, and queen but your jack guards dummy's small card on the fourth round of the suit. If you discard from this holding, you will destroy the power of the jack.

Example 17:2 Keeping protection for the queen.

> **Dummy**
> ♠ A K J 6

Partner
♠ 5 4

You
♠ Q 9 7

> **Declarer**
> ♠ 10 8 3 2

You need both of your small cards to protect the queen. If you discard from the Q-9-7, you will burn your trick. The queen needs two small cards.

You should also strive to keep two small cards with the king or the ace. The reason is not to protect your winner but to protect **partner's:**

Example 17:3 Keeping protection for the king.

> **Dummy**
> ♡ A 9 7 4

Partner
♡ Q J

You
♡ K 8 3

> **Declarer**
> ♡ 10 6 5 2

Given the chance, you can discard the eight or the three and still make a trick with your king but look at what you would do to partner — not to mention your partnership. After discarding the three, all of your partnership's honours would crash on the first two rounds of the suit, so your side would only make one trick. If you had kept your small card you would have made two. The same argument applies when discarding from the ace:

Example 17:4 Keeping protection for partner's jack.

Dummy

♡ K 6 3

Partner   **You**

♡ J 9 2   ♡ A 5 4

Declarer

♡ Q 10 8 7

Faced with an early discard or two, you might easily decide that the small cards in this suit are no use and let one go. Wrong! You have just blown a trick because you can no longer wait to trap dummy's king with your ace.

Declarer plays the three towards his queen, which you properly duck. Now he plays the seven, partner plays the nine which is ducked in dummy. If you still had the small card you could let your partner hold this trick, but since you don't, you must indelicately play the ace.

Always aim to retain at least two small cards with the ace, king, or queen, and three small cards with the jack.

KEEPING LENGTH
Retain your length in the opposition suits. When declarer or dummy have a suit of four cards or more it is important that you keep equal length, even if your holding does not appear strong.

Example 17:5 Keeping length with dummy.

Dummy
♡ A Q 8 3

Partner   **You**
♡ J 10 7   ♡ 9 5 4 2

Declarer
♡ K 6

Even when your cards are poor, you need to remain alert. Forced to make an early discard, it would be easy to discard the two from this holding, but it would be a mistake. The nine guards the fourth round of the suit in dummy and all your small cards are needed as protection. After discarding one, the ace-king-queen will exhaust you of the suit so the eight will make. If you keep all four, declarer can only make his ace-king-queen.

Keeping length is a job that only one defender can do. If dummy has four or more in the suit and you have the same length, there are not enough cards left for partner to also guard the suit. You must therefore recognise the situation.

It is equally important to keep length with *declarer's* suits, although you won't always know what they are. While dummy is exposed for all to see, the distribution of declarer's hand is not so visible.

Sometimes you will know which suits declarer holds: the bidding may tell you or the play of a suit may alert you.

Example 17:6 Keeping length with declarer.

Dummy
♠ A Q 9 3
♡ A Q 4
♢ 9 6 4 3
♣ 10 8

Partner   **You**
♢ 2 led   ♠ 8 5
                                    ♡ J 10 5 3
                                    ♢ K 8
                                    ♣ Q J 9 3 2

South opened one heart, North bid one spade and raised South's one notrump rebid to three notrumps.

On the two of diamonds you play the king which wins. You return a diamond, partner wins the ten and cashes the ace-queen, declarer having started with J x x. You have two discards to make; what are they?

It is not a good idea to void yourself in a suit that is well-held by declarer so you should hold onto your spades and part with two clubs. Partner exits with a spade and declarer proceeds to cash four tricks in the suit, having started with K-J-x. Meanwhile you have to find two discards. Should it be hearts or clubs?

Although both suits contain promising honours, you should say farewell to your club honours. Since declarer is known to have a heart suit you must keep your stopper.

This is the full layout:

```
                    Dummy
                    ♠ A Q 9 3
                    ♡ K Q 4
                    ◇ 9 6 4 3
                    ♣ 10 8
  Partner                              You
  ♠ 10 7 6 2                           ♠ 8 5
  ♡ 6                                  ♡ J 10 5 3
  ◇ A Q 10 2                           ◇ K 8
  ♣ K 6 5 4                            ♣ Q J 9 3 2
                    Declarer
                    ♠ K J 4
                    ♡ A 9 8 7 2
                    ◇ J 7 5
                    ♣ A 7
```

If you discard even one little heart, declarer will score up his unmakeable game.

KEEPING LONG SUIT WINNERS

Keep your length in suits you are establishing. There is no point in setting a suit up if you throw your winners away:

Example 17:7 Keeping long suit winners.

Contract: 3NT
Lead: ♠ 6

```
                Dummy
                ♠ A 4
                ♡ A 9 6
                ◇ A Q 8 5 2
                ♣ K 7 3

You                         Partner
♠ Q 10 8 6 2                ♠ K 9 3
♡ J 7 2                     ♡ Q 8 5 4
◇ 7 6                       ◇ 9 4 3
♣ 9 8 2                     ♣ A 10 4

                Declarer
                ♠ J 7 5
                ♡ K 10 3
                ◇ K J 10
                ♣ Q J 6 5
```

You lead the six of spades against three notrumps. Partner wins dummy's four with the king and knocks out the ace. Declarer reels off five diamonds so you must make three discards. What are they?

It is essential that you keep all your spades. Unless you take four spade tricks you cannot beat this contract. With the choice narrowed down to hearts and clubs, you should discard clubs. Although your jack of hearts is only a partial guard, it could be helpful, whereas the club suit is useless.

When declarer turns to clubs for his ninth trick, partner will step in with the ace and lead a spade for you to take your three remaining winners, defeating the contract by one trick. For this defence to succeed, you have to keep all your spades.

KEEP LENGTH IN PARTNER'S SUIT

Your small cards in the suit partner leads can play a vital role in establishing and cashing that suit.

Example 17:8 Holding on to partner's suit.

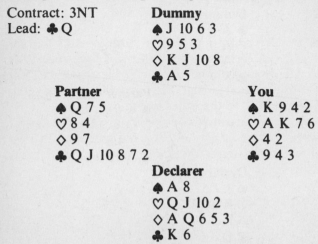

Contract: 3NT
Lead: ♣Q

Dummy
♠ J 10 6 3
♡ 9 5 3
◇ K J 10 8
♣ A 5

Partner
♠ Q 7 5
♡ 8 4
◇ 9 7
♣ Q J 10 8 7 2

You
♠ K 9 4 2
♡ A K 7 6
◇ 4 2
♣ 9 4 3

Declarer
♠ A 8
♡ Q J 10 2
◇ A Q 6 5 3
♣ K 6

Partner leads the queen of clubs against three notrumps. Declarer wins the king and plays off his five diamond tricks. Partner correctly discards a heart, a club and a spade. What do you discard? A spade, a heart, and . . .? No, not a club. You must keep your third club to lead to partner. Let go a second heart. Now when declarer plays a heart you can win the king and clear the clubs. If he plays a second heart you can win the ace and lead your last club to partner's established suit.

SIGNALLING

When discarding, you can give partner an indication of which suit you would like led. A small card says you do not want that suit led and a big card says you do. This is how it works:

Example 17:9 Indicating a lead to partner.

Your hand
♠ A Q 10 8 3
♡ 8 7 5 2
♦ 6
♣ 9 7 3

Suppose you are defending a notrump contract and partner leads a low diamond. Declarer wins and plays four rounds of clubs what do you discard on the fourth club? It should be clear from your inability to play a high diamond that you have no strength there, but what of the other two suits?

There are two ways to show your opinion: play the lowest heart to show disinterest or play the eight of spades to express enthusiasm. Most signalling is done by discouraging the suits you do not want led.

Example 17:10 Using information from a signal.

Contract: 6 ♠
Lead: ♠ 3

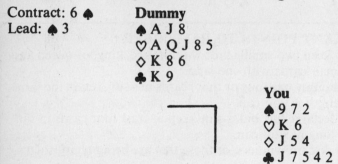

Dummy
♠ A J 8
♡ A Q J 8 5
♦ K 8 6
♣ K 9

You
♠ 9 7 2
♡ K 6
♦ J 5 4
♣ J 7 5 4 2

Partner leads a trump against six spades. Declarer wins and draws two more trumps, partner pitching the two of diamonds on the third. Declarer now leads the ten of hearts which is ducked to your king, what do you play? To beat this contract you will have to find partner with an ace, but which one?

The secret is to watch your partner's discards. He discarded the two of diamonds so he can hardly have that ace. If he has an ace it will be the ace of clubs so try a club. The full hand:

Dummy
♠ A J 8
♡ A Q J 8 5
◇ K 8 6
♣ K 9

Partner
♠ 4 3
♡ 9 7 3
◇ 10 9 7 2
♣ A 8 6 3

You
♠ 9 7 2
♡ K 6
◇ J 5 4
♣ J 7 5 4 2

Declarer
♠ K Q 10 6 5
♡ 10 4 3
◇ A Q 3
♣ Q 10

IMPORTANT POINTS TO REMEMBER
1. Aim to keep two small cards with the ace, king, or queen and three small cards with the jack.
2. When dummy has four or more cards in a suit, retain the same same length if you can.
3. When declarer has bid a suit keep at least four cards in that suit as long as you can.
4. Do not discard winners, or those that are being established as winners.
5. Do not discard in the suit partner led.
6. Play a high card to **encourage** the lead of that suit; play a low card to **discourage** the lead of that suit.

Chapter 18
MID-GAME

In this chapter you will learn the tactics of the mid-game. This includes when to change the suit and which suit to choose. Also which card to select when returning partner's suit.

The nearer you get to the end of a hand of bridge, the more you must work out what is going on. Rules may be helpful in deciding the lead but they do not begin to cover all the later situations you will face. This chapter is not an attempt to replace the vital thinking process. Instead it makes it easier by setting out guidelincs of what to think about and tips on special moves.

The mid-game is when the defenders first regain the lead. They are armed with the information from the opening lead and declarer's initial play, but nothing more.

RETURNING PARTNER'S LEAD

Unless you have good reason, return your partner's lead. This is not the instinctive play. The play that comes most naturally is to lead your **own** suit, but this is wrong. Once you start to establish one suit it pays to put your partnership effort into that suit rather than flit about.

There will be times when you will be tempted to switch to your own suit but usually you should resist. You need hard, clear evidence to make a change and even in a case like this the evidence is insufficient:

Example 18:1 Return partner's lead.

Contract: 3NT
Lead: ♡ 6

Dummy
♠ 6 3
♡ 8 5 2
♢ A Q J 9 2
♣ K 9 2

Partner
♡ 6 led

You
♠ K Q J 8 4
♡ 7 3
♢ K 8
♣ J 10 8 3

West	North	East	South
			1 ♣
pass	1 ♢	pass	1NT
pass	2NT	pass	3NT

Partner leads the six of hearts which floats to declarer's nine. At trick two the ten of diamonds is run to your king. What do you return?

It is a choice between returning hearts or shifting to spades. Either play could be the winner; partner could have the ace of spades or he could have good hearts.

Although there are no guarantees, return the original suit; lead a heart. It is more likely that partner has strong hearts, and even if you are wrong, he will be touched that you thought of him. The full layout:

Dummy
- ♠ 6 3
- ♡ 8 5 2
- ◇ A Q J 9 2
- ♣ K 9 2

Partner
- ♠ 9 7 2
- ♡ A Q 10 6 4
- ◇ 7 6 3
- ♣ 5 4

You
- ♠ K Q J 8 4
- ♡ 7 3
- ◇ K 8
- ♣ J 10 8 3

Declarer
- ♠ A 10 5
- ♡ K J 9
- ◇ 10 5 4
- ♣ A Q 7 6

The heart return through the king-jack allows partner to cash four tricks in the suit. On a spade shift, declarer will grab the ace and make his contract — four diamond tricks, one heart, one spade, and three clubs.

When returning partner's suit, lead low if you started with four and high if you started with three. In these examples, you play the queen on the first round of the suit, which holds. What do you return?

Example 18:2 Which card to return in partner's suit.

Dummy
- ♣ 5 3

Partner
- ♣ 4 led

You
- a. ♣ Q 8 6
- b. ♣ Q 9 6 2
- c. ♣ K Q 7
- d. ♣ A K Q 8
- e. ♣ K Q 8 2

SOLUTIONS:
a. Return the eight — top of the remaining doubleton
b. Return the two — having started with four
c. Return the king — top of a doubleton, unblocking as always
d. Return the ace — top of a sequence
e. Return the two — low from four cards

This information can be vital:

Example 18:3 Watching partner's spots.

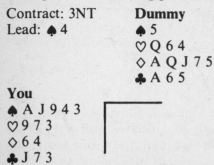

Contract: 3NT   **Dummy**
Lead: ♠ 4
    ♠ 5
    ♡ Q 6 4
    ◇ A Q J 7 5
    ♣ A 6 5

You
♠ A J 9 4 3
♡ 9 7 3
◇ 6 4
♣ J 7 3

You lead the four of spades against three notrumps. Partner comes to light with the king and returns the two. Declarer follows small as you win the nine. Declarer is marked with the queen by partner's play of the king at trick one. With the king and queen partner would have played the queen, the lowest of touching honours.

The issue is whether declarer started with Q x x x or Q x x. If he started with Q x x the queen is now bare so cash the ace to pick her up and run the suit. If he began with Q x x x, the queen is still guarded, so you will need partner to lead through again. Which do you think is the case?

It may look like guesswork, but it is not. The key is the card that partner returned. He led the two which means he started with four. You and dummy started with six spades, leaving partner and declarer with a total of seven. Since partner has shown four, declarer started with three and his queen is now bare. You can confidently play the ace to drop the queen.

Suppose partner returns the eight, declarer plays the ten, and you win the jack. What now? Once again, partner is showing you the way. The return of a high card — the eight — indicates an original holding of three, so you must try to get partner on lead. The best chance is a heart. Lead the nine of hearts, top of nothing.

TIME FOR A CHANGE, BUT WHAT?

Generally you should continue the original lead; chopping and changing suits is not a good idea. Nevertheless, there are times when you must shift suits. First you must recognise the futility of the original attack and then you must work out what to play instead.

Example 18:4 Reversing from a cul-de-sac.

Contract: 4 ♠
Lead: ♡ 5

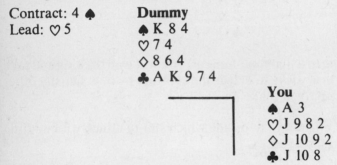

Dummy
♠ K 8 4
♡ 7 4
♢ 8 6 4
♣ A K 9 7 4

You
♠ A 3
♡ J 9 8 2
♢ J 10 9 2
♣ J 10 8

Partner leads the five of hearts; your jack is taken by declarer with the queen. A spade is played to the king and your ace. What do you return?

There is not much future in the heart suit since dummy has a doubleton. You can take one trick if partner has the ace, and none if he doesn't. It is doubtful he does because it is wrong to lead a small card in a suit that is headed by the ace against a suit contract.

The time has come to abandon hearts and try another avenue.

The clubs are too big to challenge so play a diamond. Lead the jack, the top of the sequence. The full layout:

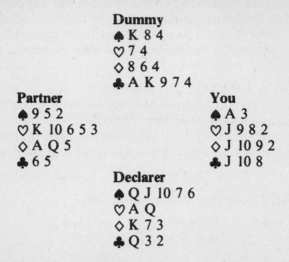

Dummy
♠ K 8 4
♡ 7 4
◇ 8 6 4
♣ A K 9 7 4

Partner
♠ 9 5 2
♡ K 10 6 5 3
◇ A Q 5
♣ 6 5

You
♠ A 3
♡ J 9 8 2
◇ J 10 9 2
♣ J 10 8

Declarer
♠ Q J 10 7 6
♡ A Q
◇ K 7 3
♣ Q 3 2

By shifting to a diamond honour, you will trap the king and take three further tricks to defeat the contract by one. On any other play declarer will make an overtrick.

You will often have to decide which suit to attack with nothing much to guide you.

Example 18:5 Leading up to weakness.

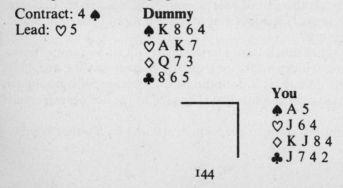

Contract: 4 ♠
Lead: ♡ 5

Dummy
♠ K 8 6 4
♡ A K 7
◇ Q 7 3
♣ 8 6 5

You
♠ A 5
♡ J 6 4
◇ K J 8 4
♣ J 7 4 2

The contract is four spades, partner leads the five of hearts which declarer wins in hand with the queen. He plays the queen of spades which you win with the ace. What do you play?

There is no future in continuing hearts so the choice is between the minor suits. With no clear indication, and dummy to your right, you should lead dummy's weakest suit; the saying is *lead up to weakness*. In this case you should lead a club. The full layout:

Dummy
♠ K 8 6 4
♡ A K 7
♢ Q 7 3
♣ 8 6 5

Partner
♠ 10 2
♡ 10 8 5 3
♢ 10 9 2
♣ A 10 9 3

You
♠ A 5
♡ J 6 4
♢ K J 8 4
♣ J 7 4 2

Declarer
♠ Q J 9 7 3
♡ Q 9 2
♢ A 6 5
♣ K Q

The club lead does nothing special, but unlike the diamond lead, it does nothing bad. Partner wins his ace and provided you play your king of diamonds when the queen is played, the contract will fail. If you shifted to a diamond, declarer would have succeeded. The diamond would have run to the queen, reducing his diamond losers from two to one.

There are two general rules to guide you in the mid-game: **lead through strength and up to weakness.**

Example 18:6 Leading through strength.

Contract: 3 ♠
Lead: ♣ 6

Dummy
♠ A K 8 6
♡ A Q 7 5
◇ 9 6 4
♣ 9 3

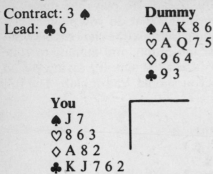

You
♠ J 7
♡ 8 6 3
◇ A 8 2
♣ K J 7 6 2

You lead a club against three spades. Partner plays the queen and declarer takes the ace. He cashes the ace and queen of spades then exits with the ten of clubs. You take the jack and . . .?

There is no absolutely clear play so you should follow general principles; lead through dummy's strength, play a heart. The full layout:

Dummy
♠ A K 8 6
♡ A Q 7 5
◇ 9 6 4
♣ 9 3

You
♠ J 7
♡ 8 6 3
◇ A 10 2
♣ K J 7 6 2

Partner
♠ 5 2
♡ K J 9 2
◇ Q J 7 5
♣ Q 8 5

Declarer
♠ Q 10 9 4 3
♡ 10 4
◇ K 8 3
♣ A 10 4

In due course partner will win the lead in hearts and he will shift to the queen of diamonds, following the principle of leading around to dummy's weakness. You can now pick up three diamond tricks by overwhelming the king to defeat the contract by one trick. If you led a diamond, declarer would have made his king and the contract.

CREATING VOIDS; EXPLOITING TRUMPS

To make the most of trumps in defence, you need a void. You will seldom be dealt a void in a side-suit so you must create if for yourself:

Example 18:7 Creating a void to secure a ruff.

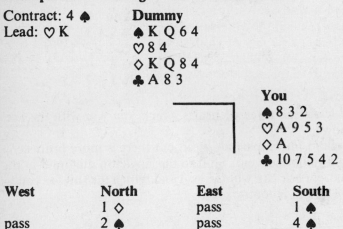

Contract: 4 ♠
Lead: ♡ K

Dummy
♠ K Q 6 4
♡ 8 4
◊ K Q 8 4
♣ A 8 3

You
♠ 8 3 2
♡ A 9 5 3
◊ A
♣ 10 7 5 4 2

West	North	East	South
	1 ◊	pass	1 ♠
pass	2 ♠	pass	4 ♠

Partner leads the king of hearts. What is your defensive plan? It looks like the defence has three tricks — two hearts and a diamond — but you need one more. You can trump a diamond but first you must cash the ace then organise for partner to lead the suit again.

You need an entry card into partner's hand so he can play a second round of diamonds and you have it in the queen of hearts;

147

the lead of the king shows the queen. You must take control. Overtake the king of hearts with the ace and cash the ace of diamonds to create the void. Now lead back a heart to partner who will work out what is going on (good old partner) and lead a diamond for you to trump. The thrill of teamwork!

You can lead a singleton to create a void:

Example 18:8 Switching to a singleton.

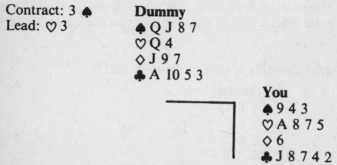

Contract: 3 ♠
Lead: ♡ 3

Dummy
♠ Q J 8 7
♡ Q 4
◊ J 9 7
♣ A 10 5 3

You
♠ 9 4 3
♡ A 8 7 5
◊ 6
♣ J 8 7 4 2

Partner leads the three of hearts which you win with the ace. What now?

You could return partner's lead but there is more promise in creating a diamond void. Shift to the singleton diamond in the hope that partner can win the lead and return the suit for you to trump. The full layout:

Dummy
♠ Q J 8 7
♡ Q 4
♦ J 9 7
♣ A 10 5 3

Partner
♠ 2
♡ K 9 6 3 2
♦ A 10 8 5 3
♣ 9 6

You
♠ 9 4 3
♡ A 8 7 5
♦ 6
♣ J 8 7 4 2

Declarer
♠ A K 10 6 5
♡ J 10
♦ K Q 4 2
♣ K Q

Partner will win the ace of diamonds and conclude that you must be short in the suit — why else would you not continue the hearts. After trumping the diamond return, switch back to hearts, partner's opening suit. This allows partner to win the king and lead another diamond for you to trump; a satisfying defence to beat the contract by one trick.

IMPORTANT POINTS TO REMEMBER:

1. Return partner's lead unless you have a good reason not to.
2. When returning partner's suit, lead high if you started with three cards and low if you started with four.
3. Play through strength and up to weakness. Lead through dummy's strong suits or around to dummy's weak suit.
4. In a suit contract, if you are short in a suit, consider leading it to create a void. The idea is that partner will return the suit before your trumps are drawn.
5. When partner changes suits in a suit contract, he could well be creating a void.

GLOSSARY

Block — A suit is blocked if winners in it cannot be taken one after another.

Break — The way the unseen cards are divided between the opponents.

Cash — To lead a card that is sure to win.

Certain tricks — Tricks that can be taken without losing the lead.

Control — Honour card in suit in which your partnership has six or less cards.

Discard — The card played when you have none in the suit led.

Danger hand — The one opponent who can cause damage if he wins the lead.

Deal — One unique layout of four hands.

Drawing trumps — The process of removing the opposition's trumps.

Ducking — Conceding a trick you could have won, in a suit in which you have length.

Entries — Cards that allow the lead to be transferred from one hand to another.

Equal honours — Honours in sequence — of adjacent rank.

Establish — The process of promoting a card to winning rank.

Exit — A losing card that is used to quit the lead.

Finesse — An attempt to take a trick with a lower-ranking card by playing after the higher-ranking card(s).

Fit — The holding in one suit between your hand and dummy. For example a 5-3 fit is five in your hand, three in dummy. A "fit" usually means a holding of eight or more in a particular suit.

Hand — A unique deal of the 52 cards — see "deal".

Hold-up play — To postpone winning a trick in a weak suit.

Honour — An ace, king, queen, or jack; sometimes a ten.

Long hand — The hand with more of a given suit (declarer or dummy).

Long suit — A suit in which you hold five or more cards.

Loser — A small card which if led would lose the trick. It is not covered by an honour or a trump in the other hand.

Mid-game — When the defenders first regain the lead.

Overtake — To play a higher card than the one already played by partner for entry reasons.

Promotion — The process of establishing secondary honours by forcing out the opposition's stoppers.

Protection — Keeping small cards so that your honours in that suit will not fall under the opposition's winners.

Ruff — To play a trump on a trick.

Secondary honour — The king, queen, jack, or ten with the higher honours missing.

Sequence — A run of two or more touching honours.

Set up — To set up is to establish.

Shift — The defenders lead a new suit.

Short hand — The hand that has less of a given suit (declarer or dummy).

Short suit — A holding of three or less cards in one suit.

Solid — A holding in a suit that contains all winners, no losers.

Spot card — Any card below the ten.

Stopper — A holding in a weak suit that will in due course take a trick.

Suit — A holding of four or more cards in one suit.

Switch — The defenders lead a new suit (same as shift).

Touching honours — Two or more honours of adjacent rank

Trump in — To play a trump on the opponent's trick.

Trump out — To clear the opposition's winners in a suit by using trumps — usually done to establish long suit tricks.

Unblocking — The process of clearing a blockage.

INDEX